Ross Montgomery

Illustrated by David Litchfield

ff

FABER & FABER

First published in 2017
by Faber and Faber Limited
Bloomsbury House,
74–77 Great Russell Street,
London, WC1B 3DA

Typeset by MRules
Printed in England by CPI Group (UK) Ltd, Croydon, CR0 4YY

A CIP record for this book
is available from the British Library

ISBN 978–0–571–31797–4

2 4 6 8 10 9 7 5 3 1

To Lian –

boo.

The good children were all in bed by now. The good children were fast asleep, tucked up in warm pyjamas and dreaming of Christmas.

But not Lewis. He wasn't one of the good children. That *was why he was trudging alone through the bitter cold to work on* Christmas *Eve.*

'Bah humbug,' he muttered.

Lewis made his way out of the village. Every doorway twinkled with fairy lights; every windowpane glowed with the warmth of a family fireplace. Lewis could see parents inside cuddled up on sofas, mantelpieces hung with stockings, hopeful children peeking down through the banisters. Every house was a Christmas box, full of wonders.

And then there was Soul's College.

It sat on the tallest hill beside the village. It was an ancient building, grim as a scorched fireplace. It glowered over the rooftops like a crow on a fence post.

That was where Lewis was spending his Christmas Eve.

'Stupid College,' he moaned. 'Stupid Mum. Stupid Dean!'

It hadn't been Lewis's idea to throw stones through the College windows – but as usual, he was the only one who got caught. The rest of his gang had scattered when the guards appeared, leaving Lewis to take the rap by himself. No one had expected there to be anyone inside

Soul's College – after all, it was the day before Christmas. The few students who still attended the crumbling old building should have left for the holidays ages ago.

The guards had dragged Lewis by the scruff of his neck through long, winding corridors to the office of the Dean – the head of Soul's College. He was a thin spike of a man, who looked exactly like the building he sat in – cold, dark and barren. He had taken Lewis in with a long, silent look . . . and smiled.

Lewis had expected him to shout – but he didn't. It was much, much worse than that. Instead, the Dean told Lewis to come back that night – Christmas Eve *night – and work for the College until he'd repaid his debt. Lewis had begged his mother to say something, but to his dismay, she'd agreed with the Dean.*

'Serves you right for spending all your time with those horrid friends of yours! You'll have to

make a choice one day, Lewis: do you want to be good, or do you want to be bad?'

Lewis reached the forest that surrounded Soul's College. It was dark inside: very dark. The air was as still as a snow globe and the ground sparkled with frost. The trees almost seemed to glow in the moonlight. Lewis took one final look at the village behind him. The old church steeple stood cold and grey on the horizon; the clock on the bell tower read half past eleven. Almost Christmas Day.

Lewis trudged up the hill, his breath curling out between his teeth in fingers. He had to admit that being asked to come to the College in the middle of the night seemed . . . well, a little strange.

But then, everything about Soul's College was strange. It had once been the best university in the country, but that was hundreds of years ago. Over the years the students had dwindled, and the building had darkened and decayed. Hardly anyone went there any more – no one even knew what went on inside.

There were rumours, of course.

Everyone at school had been talking about it for years. On Christmas Eve, when Soul's College closed and all the lights went out, something about it . . . changed. It was as if the building suddenly came alive. Those who were brave enough to stay up late and watch it – at least, those who said they did – whispered about seeing shadows at the windows. They even said that if you listened carefully enough, you could hear voices coming from inside.

No, not just voices. Screams.

Lewis shivered, and wrapped his coat tight around himself.

'Come on – it's Christmas Eve. Nothing bad can ever happen on Christmas Eve. Family, warm socks, eggnog . . .'

The hill crested, and Soul's College rose out of the ground like a gravestone.

Lewis gulped. The building seemed somehow bigger than he remembered. It was surrounded by black metal gates and a high spiked fence. There was a wooden model of Father Christmas on the roof, but it didn't seem particularly cheerful. In fact, from where Lewis was standing, it almost seemed like it was leering down at him with a malevolent grin on its face.

'Hello?' Lewis called out.

His voice went into the cold night air, and didn't come back. It was like the darkness ate it. Lewis tugged at his scarf nervously.

'It's Christmas Eve,' he repeated. 'Nothing bad can happen on Christmas Eve.'

He stepped bravely through the gates and made his way to the dining hall, just as the Dean had told him to. It was big and cold and empty inside. There was a fire at one end that gave no warmth, and a high ceiling lost to darkness. The walls hung with heavy tapestries.

In the centre of the room was a long dining table, set for fifty guests.

So that was it – the College was holding a dinner. Lewis was going to work as a serving boy. But it didn't look *like a dinner was about to start any time soon – especially not a Christmas one. No one could be festive in a room as cold and miserable as this. The only sign it was Christmas at all was the scraggly tree beside the fireplace, decorated with a sorry string of tinsel and seven sad baubles.*

Lewis gazed at the enormous portrait hanging above the mantelpiece. It was the only part of the room that was warm and friendly. Lewis knew the man in the painting – everyone in the village did. It was Lord Caverner, the man who had built Soul's College hundreds of years ago. He'd been much loved in his time, and it was easy to see why: he had a warm, kind face, with a thick beard and a smile that reached his eyes. Lewis felt safer just looking at him.

'Come on – it's Christmas Eve. Nothing bad could ever happen on Christmas E—'

Creak.

A door had opened at the other end of the room. Lewis turned round . . . but there was no one there. The far wall was lost to darkness.

'Hello?'

Nothing – the room was silent.

Then – ever so quietly – Lewis heard something move. The steady scrape of dead feet on flagstones, one after the other. They grew out of the darkness, getting closer.

Then they stopped.

Lewis stood still, his breath held in his throat.

There was someone standing in the darkness in front of him.

Lewis couldn't see their face . . . but he could make out their shape. They were hunched double, as if they were in terrible pain. Their chest swelled and shuddered with every breath.

'What are you doing here?'

The voice was hoarse and rasping: it sounded like it hurt just coming out of them. Lewis swallowed hard.

'I–I'm supposed to work here tonight.' He glanced at the table. 'For the Christmas dinner?'

The man convulsed. He gave a high, hacking cough that was almost a laugh . . . then stepped into the firelight. Lewis could finally see his face.

But it wasn't a face.

The man had no lips. He had no eyelids. His skin was like cold, cooked meat packed into clumps against his skull. He wore ragged overalls, streaked with blood and grease. On top of his head was a high white chef's hat.

'Like Christmas, do you boy?'

Lewis didn't answer – he couldn't speak. There was nothing he could do, nothing except stand frozen to the spot in terror. The Cook came slouching out of the darkness, his red eyes boggling in their lidless sockets.

'I said: do – you – like – Christmas?'

Lewis had no idea what the Cook wanted – but he had a sickening feeling that something terrible would happen if he didn't do whatever he asked. He nodded frantically.

'Good,' *said the Cook.* 'Then listen to everything I say – that is, if you want to live to see Christmas morning.'

Lewis gasped. The Cook leaned in close – close enough for Lewis to smell the years of cooking which clung to him like ghosts.

'They're coming, boy. They'll be here any moment. Don't talk to them. Don't speak at all if you can help it. And for pity's sake, boy – DON'T MAKE THEM ANGRY.'

Lewis's mind reeled. 'Th–them? What do you mean, them . . .'

Outside, a smash of glass – Lewis spun round. The building wasn't empty any more – oh no. It was surrounded. He could hear things moving towards the dining room from all sides, growing louder, getting closer. Crashes, bangs, wheels on gravel . . . Lewis could hear voices, too.

But they sounded like screams.

'Get ready, boy,' *said the Cook.* 'Our guests have arrived.'

The doors burst open and a belt of freezing wind flooded the dining room.

Lewis screamed as a motorcycle roared through the doors towards him. He only just managed to throw himself out the way before it flew past and smashed into a trophy cabinet. The rider had leapt off at the last second, and now stood smoking a cigar and surveying the damage with a grin.

'Bullseye!' he said proudly. 'Got it in one!'

'Bullseye? Pah!' came another voice at the

door. 'You're losing your touch, Bloodrick – you missed the serving boy this time!'

A woman was heaving herself through the doorway. She was the biggest, foulest, most disgusting woman Lewis had ever laid eyes on. She wore a mouldy fur coat, and a hat made of rotting thistles slumped over her head. She was surrounded by a pack of ravenous hounds that roared and snapped and pulled viciously at their chains. She yanked Lewis to his feet.

'Look at him! Scrawny as a gnat and twice as ugly! He won't last till morning!'

CRAAAAASH.

The stained-glass window exploded behind them, and an enormous black horse flew through the air. It landed on the table like a ton of bricks, shattering the glassware and stamping the china to dust. Riding high on its back was a woman with a pinched, cruel face and glasses so thick her eyes looked like holes drilled straight into her skull.

'Miss Ariadne Biter!' said the enormous woman, shoving Lewis aside. 'What an entrance – you look even more revolting than usual!'

The woman flashed a hungry smile. 'And you, Lady Arabella Dogspit. Another meeting upon us already – has it really *been a whole year since last Christmas?'*

'AAAAAAARGH!'

The fireplace erupted in a cloud of soot and smoke and something flew out of the chimney, smashing off three walls and thumping into Lewis's chest so hard he was knocked off his feet once more. He looked down at the smoking heap in his hands . . . and screamed.

It was a burnt and blackened head, its mouth stretched open in a sickening smile. Lewis flung it away as fast as he could and scrambled across the floor . . .

Then stopped. It wasn't a real head – it was from the wooden model of Father Christmas on the roof. Someone had ripped it off and flung it down the chimney. Next to come was his sack of presents, big round belly, and finally a short squat man who burst out of the fireplace, quite clearly on fire, before leaping out of the window and throwing himself, bum first, into a snowdrift.

'Retch Wallmanner – you absolute goon!' cried Bloodrick. 'Every year, the same entrance . . . and look! He's gone and put the fire out, too!'

Miss Biter cackled. 'Well then, we'd better stoke it up, hadn't we?'

She pointed to the Christmas tree beside the fireplace, and the three guests howled with delight. They threw themselves at it, tearing the tree to pieces and cramming it into the fire like a murder victim. The miserable tree caught alight instantly. The flames rose higher and higher, *stretching the shadows of the guests up the walls like demons.*

'DOWN WITH CHRISTMAS,' *they cried,* 'AND LONG LIVE THE CHRISTMAS DINNER OF SOULS!'

Lewis looked around the hall in disbelief. More and more guests were arriving every second. They came tunnelling up through the flagstones, clambering through the shattered windows, smashing motorcars through the walls. They were the most hideous people Lewis had ever seen in his life – each one seemed even more unwashed, loud and foul than the last.

Lewis had no idea what was going on – but he knew one thing for certain. He didn't want to be in Soul's College any more. He wanted to be back home in his safe warm bed, as far away from these horrible people as possible. He shot to the exit—

'Oi! *Where do you think* you're *going?*'

A bony hand clamped round Lewis's wrist and

dragged him back. Standing before him was a man in a filthy pinstripe suit and broken bowler hat, glaring down at him through a black-rimmed monocle.

'What's that you've you got there, Sir Algernon?' someone cried. 'An intruder?'

The man grinned. 'Even better – a serving boy!'

Lewis was suddenly surrounded by shrieking guests, grabbing and pinching and shoving him.

'A serving boy!'

'Pull out his hair!'

'Scratch his face!'

'Break his little arms!'

'LET – HIM – GO,' *a voice roared.*

The guests released Lewis at once, and he swung round. Standing in the doorway, glaring with fury, was the Dean.

'WHAT IS THE MEANING OF THIS?'

The guests backed away – even the dogs started whining. The Dean stormed towards them, his face outraged. Lewis could have cried with relief. The nightmare was finally over; these so-called guests would be thrown out, Lewis would be sent home, and everything would be safe and sound once more . . .

‘How many times have I told you?’ the Dean cried. ‘No one is allowed to harm the serving boy until after *the Christmas Dinner of Souls has finished!’*

Lewis’s face fell. The Dean walked straight past him.

‘You can damage the College all you wish – smash the plates, stamp on the glasses, spit on the paintings until you’re red in the face – but you know the rules! The serving boy must *be kept alive until the night is over!’*

The Dean reached for the portrait hanging above the fireplace.

‘For heaven’s sake – do you know nothing *of tradition?’*

He flipped over the painting with one sweep of his arms. Lewis gasped. There was another picture secretly hidden on the other side – but the man in this portrait was nothing like Lord Caverner. This man was tall and thin, with mad pale eyes and filthy grey hair. He looked as though he had lived in darkness all his life.

And right where his mouth should have been, there was nothing. Someone had ripped the canvas from the painting, leaving a jagged hole that stretched from his jawbone to his heart. In its place, a single polished plaque read:

EDGAR CAVERNER

'We follow Edgar's rules to a tee!' barked the Dean. 'Without him, there would be no Christmas Dinner of Souls!' He turned to the guests. 'And what are the rules?'

Hands shot up on every side.

'Dinner begins at midnight!'

'Seven guests must tell a story!'

'No one may leave until the winner has entered the Catacombs!'

'And no one touches the serving boy until after the Dinner is complete.' The Dean grinned. 'Then we all know what happens to the serving boy – don't we?'

He turned to Lewis and gave a long, loud cackle. Soon all the guests were joining in, howling with laughter and rubbing their hands with hideous glee. Lewis trembled from head to toe. The Cook was right. If he did anything that these maniacs didn't like . . . he'd never get out of Soul's College alive.

A tall black clock struck the hour: twelve chimes, filling the room like a death rattle.

'The dead of midnight!' cried the Dean. 'The hour has come – our Christmas Dinner of Souls begins!'

The guests shrieked with delight and fought for the chairs around the dining table. It was already covered in shattered glass and spilled wine, but the guests didn't seem to notice or care.

'Boy! Serve us!'

The Dean pointed to a cabinet in the corner, shaped like a black coffin and filled with shelf after shelf of bottled gin. Before Lewis could respond the guests rained down plates and cutlery on his head.

'Didn't you hear him?'

'We want gin, you filthy rat!'

'Faster, maggot!'

Lewis didn't need telling twice. He grabbed two bottles and raced round the table, pouring out gin for the guests with trembling hands. They knocked it back like water and sent their glasses smashing into the fireplace.

'So!' announced the Dean. 'Once more, our secret society holds its annual Christmas Dinner of Souls! Once again, we gather at darkest midnight to continue the tradition started over two hundred years ago by our lord and founder, Edgar Caverner!'

The Dean turned to the mouthless painting behind him and the table fell into respectful silence.

'Edgar was always destined for great things,' said the Dean. 'His father, Lord Caverner, wanted a son who was good and kind . . . but Edgar was born evil. He ate every pet rabbit his father bought him! Set fire to his schoolbooks

and burned down a hospital! And more than anything, he hated Christmas. Abhorred it. Despised it!' The Dean grimaced. 'The tinsel, the presents, the singing . . .'

The guests booed and retched and made unspeakable gestures. The Dean waved them quiet.

'So Edgar hatched a plan. Once a year, on Christmas Eve, he would sneak into his little sisters' rooms and tell them stories so horrifying, so disgusting, that they would be too frightened to sleep. They'd spend Christmas Day rigid with terror, weeping into their stockings. Soon, the merest mention of Christmas made them burst into tears. Eventually Lord Caverner had no choice but to ban it from the household entirely. Young Edgar had won – he'd ruined Christmas!'

'DOWN WITH CHRISTMAS!' the guests cheered, drumming on the table and smashing what was left of the plates.

Lewis was horrified. What was wrong with these people? How on earth could they hate Christmas?

'*When Edgar was older,' the Dean continued, 'Lord Caverner sent him away to Soul's* College. *He hoped that studying at his world-famous university might finally put Edgar on the straight and narrow . . . but he was wrong! It was in* this very room *that Edgar held the first Christmas Dinner of Souls, a place for all those who despised Christmas to gather each year and tell the most spine-chilling stories they knew. But* no one *was a match for Edgar! There was no one more unpleasant, more terrifying, more disgusting than he!'*

The Dean raised his glass.

'He *is the reason we spend the rest of the year working in this rotten, stinking university – to be near the legend of the greatest horror-storyteller who ever lived. A toast – to Edgar Caverner!'*

Lewis's eyes widened – he finally understood. These weren't just any guests – they were the teachers and lecturers of Soul's College. No wonder the College had fallen from grace over the years: these awful people had transformed it into a monstrous clubhouse.

'BOY! Where's our gin?'

'Worthless, cack-handed runt!'

A plate flew past Lewis's head. He gasped – he'd let his thoughts drift, just for a second. He ran round the table, pouring out two more bottles as fast as he could. If he wanted to survive the night, he was going to have to stay on his toes.

'Then,' said the Dean, 'one fateful Christmas night . . . Edgar had a dream.'

The guests fell silent. The Dean leaned over the table.

'In the dream, he was the Lord of Darkness – and he had the power to destroy Christmas. He rode high above the rooftops in a pitch-black sleigh, *leaping down chimneys to whisper bloodcurdling stories into children's ears. They would wake up screaming and wet the bed with fright.* Christmas *Day became a day to be feared. Soon it was wiped from the face of the earth completely . . . and all thanks to Edgar.'*

The Dean leaned even further across the table, his voice barely a whisper.

'And in the dream, there was only one thing which gave him the power to do it: the rotting teeth he wore inside his mouth. The Dead Man's Jabberers.'

The dining room was as silent as a graveyard now, the guests hanging on the Dean's every word.

'Legend spoke of a set of teeth that gave whoever wore them the power to tell terrifying stories. Not just any *stories – stories so frightening that they could send a man insane. Stories frightening enough to kill. Stories*

which – in the right hands – could fill the world with darkness.

'Of course, everyone knew the teeth didn't really exist. They were just a myth – a fairy tale made to frighten children. Some said they were once the teeth of an evil Viking warlord, plucked from his corpse by a witch doctor and bound together with curses. Some said they were the teeth of the Devil himself. But from the moment Edgar woke up, he knew he had to find them. They were the key to his dream – to finally destroy Christmas, once and for all!'

Lewis gasped. Surely the Dean wasn't serious – surely no one would want to take the rotting teeth from a corpse and put them into their mouth?

'Edgar stopped going to lectures,' said the Dean. 'He stopped sleeping. All he did, night and day, was search the College library for information about the Jabberers. He found stories of them from hundreds of years ago. He *discovered that whoever wore the teeth would live forever – unless someone killed them and claimed the teeth for themselves. He discovered that if the teeth considered you unworthy, the second you put them in your mouth they would bite out your tongue and kill you instantly!*

'But he found no proof that the teeth actually existed. Every clue to their whereabouts quickly became a dead end. He found reported sightings in Scotland, in Peru, in darkest Antarctica – all rumours. It seemed that the Dead Man's Jabberers might really be a myth. Edgar began to despair.

'Then one day, news reached the College of a demonic figure terrorising villagers in Siberia. No one believed the stories: after all, they sounded too ludicrous to be true. Terrified villagers were saying that someone was breaking into people's houses in the middle of the night and frightening them to death. *A man who could kill people just by telling them stories – a man with rotting teeth.*

'Edgar wasted no time: he stole as much of his father's money as he could, leapt on the nearest train and set out for darkest Siberia. This was his one chance to find the Dead Man's Jabberers, claim them for himself, and use their power to destroy Christmas once and for all . . . !'

The Dean let his last words hang in the air, echoing off the chamber walls. When he spoke again, it was with a whisper.

'And that, of course, is the last time anyone saw Edgar alive. His body was found two years later, floating face down in the black waters of the Volga. No one knows how he died. Perhaps the teeth killed him – perhaps someone else did. No one knows for certain. No one knows because Lord Caverner paid an unspeakable amount of money to have his son's body transported back to Soul's College before anyone could inspect it, and secretly buried him in the Catacombs beneath our feet.'

The Dean stepped to one side and lifted up a rug on the floor. Sunk into the stone of the floor was a thick iron trapdoor, deadbolted ten times over. Carved across the middle was one word:

CATACOMBS

'No one could understand why Lord Caverner chose to bury his only son here instead of in the family crypt. The Catacombs are a huge maze: you could search down there for days and never find what you were looking for. It was a privilege reserved for old College staff: a way to protect their coffins from bodysnatchers. Why on earth would Lord Caverner want to hide his son's body where no one could ever find it . . . ?'

The Dean swung round, a glint in his eye.

'The reason is obvious: Edgar was wearing the Dead Man's Jabberers when he died, and Lord

Caverner wanted to make sure no one found out the truth! And if that wasn't proof enough, the last thing he did before he left the College, never to return, was find this *painting of his son and rip out the mouth with his bare hands!'*

Lewis looked up at the painting. It seemed like it was alive somehow, staring down at the guests with its pale eyes and sucking all the light from the room into its gaping mouth.

'Tonight,' said the Dean, 'we continue the tradition which Edgar started and gather for another Christmas Dinner of Souls. But we're not simply competing to tell the scariest story! We're competing to find someone worthy of taking Edgar's place. Someone scary enough to venture into the Catacombs, find his body and pluck the Dead Man's Jabberers from his skull. Someone who can finally wipe Christmas from the face of the earth, once and for all!'

Lewis gasped. He couldn't believe his

ears – was that *what was going on here tonight? These people were plotting to destroy* Christmas?

'Since Edgar's death,' said the Dean, 'over two hundred guests have descended into the Catacombs to search for his body. No one has ever returned. Tonight, we will pick one more storyteller to look for the Dead Man's Jabberers. If they are worthy of the teeth, they will become our new Lord of Darkness – if not, the teeth will bite out their tongue and kill them instantly!'

The guests shuffled in their chairs. Lewis could see in every one of their mean, greedy eyes how much they longed for the chance to wear the Dead Man's Jabberers – but that they feared winning as much as they desired it.

The Dean stepped towards the fireplace and picked up a set of black metal tongs. He reached into the heart of the flames and brought out a single scorched bauble.

'Tonight, seven guests have been selected from

your ranks. They've each had a year to prepare their story.'

He held up the bauble. The fire had burned away its top layer: beneath it the paper was black as night, with a white skull painted above a blood-red number.

'Each guest will serve a specially made course to accompany their tale,' said the Dean. 'When the night is over and all seven stories have been told, a winner will be chosen to search for Edgar's tomb.'

The Dean picked out six more baubles from the flames and placed them in a row on the table.

'Once the winner has descended into the Catacombs . . . the night is over! Everyone must leave and wait to see whether or not Christmas morning comes . . . to discover if our new Lord of Darkness has risen!' The Dean grinned. 'Everyone, of course, except . . . for the serving boy.'

He turned to Lewis, his eyes sparkling.

'Because we all know what happens to the serving boy, don't we?'

The guests burst into maniacal laughter once more, hooting and slapping the table. Lewis's legs shook – it was no good. He couldn't stay here a moment longer. These monstrous people were going to kill him – and not only that, they were going to destroy Christmas! He had to get out and find a way to stop them, before it was too late!

He fled for the door, but the only exit was blocked by Lady Arabella's dogs. They roared and snapped at him, driving him back to the table as the guests howled with laughter.

'There is no escape, boy!' cried the Dean. 'The Christmas Dinner of Souls has already begun!'

The Dean lifted the first of the seven baubles and smashed it on the table. A swarm of steaming maggots poured out, scuttling across the table as quickly as they could before the guests could eat them. The Dean pulled a slither of paper from the glass fragments and held it above him.

'Our first storyteller of the night is . . . Lady Arabella Dogspit! Our esteemed Professor of Blood Oaths and Curses!'

The enormous woman who had grabbed Lewis earlier stood up to rapturous applause. The door to the kitchen swung open in a cloud of rank steam, and the Cook stepped into the dining room holding a great silver platter.

Lewis's stomach heaved. In the centre of the platter lay a huge roasted fish, with grey sunken eyes and a rack of razor-sharp teeth. But this was no ordinary fish: it stood on top of eight spidery legs, each one thick with bristling hair and ending with a cloven hoof. A set of spiked, gleaming horns curled out of its brow and glistened in the firelight.

'Well?' *cried the Dean. 'What are you waiting for, boy? Bring it to the table!'*

Lewis didn't move – the thought of being anywhere near *the fish made him want to be sick . . .*

But then he saw the look in the Cook's eye. A *warning.*

Don't make them angry.

The Cook *was right – if Lewis wanted to find a way out of here, then he had to stay alive. He quickly took the platter and heaved it onto the table in front of Lady Arabella Dogspit. She dragged the stinking fish towards her and smiled at the guests.*

'This,' *she said, 'is an Abyssinian Striker Trout. It lives at the bottom of the darkest lakes, hiding in the mud where no one can see it. Then . . . it waits. It waits until a moonless night has come and crawls onto land, so it can feast on any foolish campers sleeping nearby!'*

She plunged a pudgy fist into the grey meat and pulled out a bone the size of a bear claw. She turned it in her hands, studying it idly.

'It suits my story perfectly: a Christmas *tale from long ago and far away, when the world was a very different place. A tale of murder most foul, and* dreadful *revenge.'*

She thrust the fish to the centre of the table and the guests launched onto it like hyenas. Lady Arabella wiped her oily hands on her dress and began her terrible story.

An Old Forgotten Scream

There was once a young and wealthy baron. He had everything you could ever wish for: youth, good looks, more money than most people could spend in a lifetime. But there was one thing the Baron didn't have: *land*. He longed for his own forests and fields, his own rivers and lakes – and the Baron was prepared to do *anything* to get them.

It so happened that there was a young lady

who was in love with the Baron. She was too besotted to see that beneath his good looks, the Baron was greedy and cruel – and that he utterly detested her. In truth, there was no one the Baron liked much apart from himself.

But the Baron *did* like the Lady's land. She owned miles and miles of it: fields as fertile as you could hope for, forests stretching long into the wilderness. You could walk for weeks without reaching the other side, nor see a single other soul along the way. The Baron was desperate to have the lands for himself – but there was no way he could do so without marrying the Lady first.

One Christmas Eve, the Baron sat unhappily in his mansion, gazing out of the window and lamenting his fate.

'Life is so unfair!' he cried. 'If only there was some way I could have that land without being married to that *idiot* for the rest of my life . . .'

Just then, the Baron noticed the fountain in his courtyard. It was a particularly cold winter, and the water had frozen to solid ice. The fish in the fountain had all died.

And just like that, the Baron came up with an evil, sickening plan to get exactly what he wanted.

He wasted no time and went straight to the Lady's castle. He got down on one knee the second he found her.

'Dear Lady, I love you! Your face is as fair and beautiful as, er . . . mine. Let's get married! And for our honeymoon, let's travel through your beautiful lands – just the two of us!'

The Lady thought her heart might burst with happiness, and the very next day she and the Baron were married. On Christmas morning the newlyweds set off on a cherry-red sleigh together as the Lady's family and servants waved them goodbye. Normally she would be accompanied by her guards, but the Baron had *insisted* that it just be the two of them. Everyone agreed this was hopelessly romantic – the Baron and the Lady had never looked happier.

Of course, no one knew the *real* reason why the Baron was smiling.

They rode for seven straight days and seven straight nights through the Lady's land. Winter had turned bitter, and the ground was as hard as stone. Icicles hung from the trees like fangs, shattering the frozen branches as they fell.

'My darling – it is terribly cold,' the Lady said with a shiver. 'Could I wear your coat?'

'No need, sweetums!' the Baron insisted. 'It's just a little further!'

They kept riding. Soon the Lady was so cold and tired she thought she might faint – but every time she asked the Baron to stop, he refused. Finally, on the seventh day, the Baron stopped beside a beautiful frozen lake, surrounded by a ring of treacherous mountains. They were miles away from the nearest village now. The land was blanketed in snow and silence.

'Almost there, tiddlykins!' said the Baron. 'But first, let's take a scenic stroll across this frozen lake.'

The Lady's teeth were chattering and her face was almost blue – but she loved her new husband too much to refuse him. She took his arm and the two of them walked across the thick black ice.

'Oh, snugglewump,' said the Baron. 'You look even more beautiful than usual today – gaze at your reflection in the ice and see for yourself!'

The Lady knelt down without question – and quick as a whip, the Baron grabbed her hair and smashed her head through the ice. She was too shocked and exhausted to fight back – all the Lady could do was scream. She screamed and screamed into the freezing water, but no one heard her except for the fish and the pondweed.

Soon she stopped screaming entirely, and slumped against the ice. She was dead.

The Baron filled her wedding gown with rocks and tossed her into the water, then strolled back to the sleigh whistling a merry tune. He looked like someone in the middle of a Boxing Day walk instead of someone who had just murdered his wife. He muddied his face, ripped his clothes, and rode for seven straight days and seven straight nights until he burst through the castle doors in floods of tears.

'There's been a terrible accident – the Lady is dead! We were riding along a mountain pass when a fearsome bear leapt out and attacked her ... I bravely fought off the beast as best I could, but he carried her away and ate her alive! Oh, tragedy – how ever will I live without my Lady? Not even the deeds to all her lands – which as her husband I now rightly inherit – can ease the pain in my heart!'

No one dared to question the Baron's story – after all, no one could prove he was lying. All the Lady's land became his, and her household went into mourning. On the day of her funeral, the Baron himself led the procession, weeping into a black lace handkerchief and negotiating the final terms of the deal with a team of mourning accountants.

Secretly, the Baron's heart sang for joy. His plan had worked perfectly – and no one would ever find out the truth.

The very next day he moved into the

Lady's castle and raised taxes, driving the nearby peasants into poverty and forcing them off her lands. He used the money to build a second castle for himself at the other end of the Lady's estate, even more luxurious than the first. Finally the Baron ordered every bear for miles around to be slaughtered in revenge for his Lady's death, and turned their fur into delightful rugs to decorate his plush new bedroom. A long, dark winter settled across the Lady's land: the Baron had never been happier.

Then one day – on the very first day of spring, in fact – the Baron awoke to a strange sound.

It was a scream – a faint, faraway scream. It seemed to be coming from outside. And stranger still, the Baron felt somehow that he *recognised* it.

He looked out of his bedroom window.

From that height he could see all the Lady's land, stretching right up to the treacherous ring of mountains on the horizon. Sure enough, the Baron could hear a scream on the wind – growing louder as it blew harder, and softer when it fell.

The Baron's blood froze in his veins. It was the Lady's scream – and it was coming from the lake where he had killed her.

'It . . . it can't be!' he cried. 'She's dead! I killed her myself!'

The Baron *knew* that the Lady couldn't be alive – but just to make sure, he sent all his soldiers to search the lands. They found nothing, of course – they even went to the very same lake where the Baron had killed her, but her body was safely hidden beneath the water.

'Mmph – how strange,' said the Baron. 'It must have been my imagination.'

But the Baron was wrong. It *wasn't* his imagination.

You see, when the Lady died she let out a scream filled with so much anger and sadness that it spread through the lake like a bloodstain. It entered the fish that swam in the water, and the plants that grew at the bottom, and the beetles that scuttled through the mud. It had stayed frozen in the lake all winter – but now the ice was melting. The scream was coming out.

Now, whenever a tadpole grew in the water and became a frog, it would emerge not with a croak, but a scream. Whenever a lily pad grew from the bottom of the lake and opened up its flower, it opened with a scream. Soon, the scream seeped into the forest soil around the lake. Trees for miles around drank up all the misery and rage of the dying Lady and grew strong with hate. When the spring buds opened, they opened with a scream on their branches, and every autumn leaf fell screaming.

The scream spread across the land like a plague, clawing its way towards the castle. The once-fertile fields became barren; crops failed and fruit withered on the tree. People began to mutter that things had started to turn bad the day that the Baron had taken over – there were even rumours that he was going mad. Why else would he send out soldiers to search for his *dead wife*?

But the Baron didn't notice what anyone was saying. He was too busy listening to the scream that seemed to be drawing closer to the castle with every passing day.

'Can't you *hear* that?' he asked his servants. 'That sound in the air?'

The servants stared at him with confusion. 'All we hear is birdsong, Your Grace.'

It was true. No one else could hear the scream except the Baron – and soon it was *all* he could hear. It was like an army approaching the castle on every side, growing louder and louder. The Baron stopped going outside – he even started to pad the cracks in his bedroom door with blankets to stop the scream from getting inside. But whenever the wind blew hardest, the Baron could swear he'd still hear the faintest trickle of a scream leak through the edge of the windowpanes.

Finally, after months of torture, the Baron couldn't take it any longer. He called all his advisors to his bedroom and made an announcement.

'I'm moving away from this horrible place! I'm going to live in my new castle at the other end of the country – and I'm never coming back!'

His advisors shared a worried glance. The

Baron's behaviour had been increasingly strange for months, and was only getting stranger.

'Well … it *is* almost Christmas,' they muttered to each other. 'It'll be the first anniversary of his wife's death soon. Oh, poor Baron – how he must have loved her!'

The very next day, the Baron packed up his belongings and left for his new castle. As his carriage moved further and further away from the mountain ring, he realised that the scream was getting quieter. He sighed with relief.

'Thank goodness! There's no *way* that the scream can follow me – my new castle is hundreds of miles away!'

The Baron arrived at the castle on Christmas Eve and had his first peaceful sleep in months, snuggled under his new bear-fur blankets. He woke on Christmas morning in high spirits and came to the breakfast table. A delicious Christmas meal was spread out before him, and pride of place in the middle of the table was the Baron's favourite meal: a whole roasted fish, smothered in herbs and butter. The Baron smacked his lips, sank a knife into the soft white flesh—

And leapt back in terror. The fish on his plate was screaming. The sound filled the room like a tide of blood, pounding against the walls and ringing in his ears. It was as if the dead Lady herself was there, screaming into the Baron's face, closer than she had ever been before.

'Wh–where did this fish come from?' the Baron cried.

The servants were bewildered – after all, they could hear nothing.

'From your own lands, sir. There were no more fish in the rivers after the harvest turned bad – your hunters had to trek for seven days and seven nights before they found a lake that still had fish in it. It was beautiful! Miles away from anyone, surrounded by a ring of mountains . . .'

The Baron threw his plate across the room.

'No! I don't want it! Burn it! Bury it! From now on, I'll cook my own meals!'

He fled the room and locked himself in the tallest tower. The servants were perplexed at the Baron's bizarre behaviour.

'He's really lost it this time,' they muttered. 'Whoever heard of burying a fish?'

The Baron didn't sleep a wink that night – instead, he stayed up until dawn and hatched a new plan. In the morning he called every one of his servants and counsellors together again.

'I can't stay here any longer,' he explained, his hands shaking and his face as pale as death. 'The scream will always find me! There's only one thing I can do – leave the country and travel overseas! There's no *way* that the infernal scream can catch up with me that way! Pack your things – we're taking the next boat to Australia!'

His advisors and servants stared at each other in shock. They turned to face the Baron – and screamed.

The Baron scrambled out of his chair.

'NO! NO, IT CAN'T BE!'

It was. His servants hadn't brought one fish with them – they'd brought dozens. After all, it was the Baron's favourite meal. And since the Baron didn't want them any more, the household had spent all Christmas Day feasting on them. Baked fish, boiled fish, dried fish, fried fish . . . Every one of them had filled their bellies with the scream, and now it coursed through their blood like oxygen.

The Baron ran from the room in terror. Each and every person he passed turned to him and let out the final bloodcurdling screams of his murdered wife. There was no escaping it; it had spread everywhere. The Baron flew to the stables and jumped on his finest horse, galloping away as fast as he could.

'I don't want her land any more! I'll live the rest of my life as a pauper! I'll do anything, *anything* to escape that horrible scream—'

The Baron never finished his sentence. He was so blinded by panic that he failed to notice the hole in the ground ahead, and his horse stumbled. The Baron flew off its back, struck his head against a rock and died instantly.

His servants found his body and carried it back to the castle. They lay him on a table and covered him in flowers. In death, the Baron finally looked peaceful.

'What a tragic end!' sighed one of his advisors. 'Driven mad by grief for his lost Lady love!'

'At least now they're together again,' said another. 'Such a pity that they never found her body – I'm sure the Baron would love to be buried alongside her!'

A third advisor was suddenly struck by a charming thought.

'Well, let's do the next best thing – we'll find the most beautiful spot on the Lady's estate and bury him there. That way the Baron will be surrounded by her spirit – for all eternity!'

Everyone agreed this was just what the Baron would have wanted.

So it was that the Baron's body was carried back to the old castle, placed on a sleigh, and driven through the Lady's lands. The burial train travelled for seven straight days and seven straight nights, until they found the perfect spot for the Baron's final resting place: a frozen lake, surrounded by a ring of mountains, miles away from anyone.

'Just what the Baron would have wanted!' said his advisors. 'And look, even the animals have even turned out to pay their last respects!'

It was true – standing beside the lake were hundreds and hundreds of animals. They stood perfectly still, watching in silence as the Baron's coffin arrived. It was almost as if they had been waiting for him.

'It's the Lady's spirit, welcoming back her beloved Baron!' said an advisor. 'How romantic!'

They dug the grave and lowered the coffin inside. The animals watched closely, their ears pricked. They were listening to the sound that none of the mourners could hear: the scream that came from the mouth of the grave as it swallowed up the coffin and sealed it in darkness forever.

The mourners left without looking back.

They didn't see the trees behind them bend and strain in the wind as their branches clawed towards the Baron's grave. They didn't see the roots beneath the ground push through the soil and wrap round his coffin like a strangled grip. They didn't see the worms and maggots chew through the wood in their thousands, pouring inside the coffin to feast on the Baron and flood his open mouth. No one saw the land take its revenge for the murdered Lady.

So it is with cruel and unjust deaths. The Lady's spirit had lived on until the Baron had paid for his crimes; now he was dead, she could finally be at peace.

But there was no peace for the Baron. There was another type of eternity for him now.

Deep beneath the earth … the Baron opened his eyes. He was trapped inside a pitch-black coffin, crushed beneath a ton of black soil. His body was writhing with maggots; he was part of the land he'd always wanted. There was no escape for him now: nothing but pain and darkness, forever and ever and ever.

The Baron opened his mouth, and screamed.

The guests cheered and clapped as Lady Arabella Dogspit finished her story. They had stripped the fish to bone with their bare hands, and were covered from head to toe in slimy scales. Lewis was horrified – he had never heard such an awful story.

'A marvellous start, Lady Arabella!' cried the Dean. 'It will take something special to beat that – but the night is still young! Boy, bring us the next course!'

Lewis didn't waste any more time – he

grabbed the empty fish tray before anyone could take a swipe at him and ran to the kitchen.

You have to find the Cook, *thought Lewis, his mind racing.* He's the only one who can help you get out of this horrible place, before it's too late!

He pushed open the kitchen door and nearly fell back. The kitchen was filled with burning gas hobs and roasting fires, and the air inside was as hot as a furnace. The Cook was hunched over a metal workstation, putting the final touches to his next dish. Lewis ran up to him.

'Please, Cook – *you have to help! Those evil people are going to kill me – we have to stop them!'*

But the Cook simply thrust the next course into Lewis's hands: another silver tray, covered with a metal domed lid.

'Quick, boy,' *he said.* 'They don't like to be kept waiting.'

'But—'

The Cook shoved Lewis back through the doors, hard, just as the clock struck one. The Dean smashed a second bauble and held up the name inside.

'Our next storyteller is Retch Wallmanner – Head Lecturer in the Satanic Arts!'

A guest leapt to his feet at the end of the table. It was the short bald man Lewis had seen flying out of the chimney earlier. He was like a firework trapped in a man's body, with eyes wild and wired as burst plugs.

'Thank you, Dean!' He shot Lady Arabella Dogspit a pointed look. 'My story is no fairy tale – it is a personal one, taken from my own family history!'

Lady Arabella Dogspit glared at him. Wallmanner gave her a smirk before turning on Lewis.

'Well, boy? Serve up!'

Lewis placed the tray on the table and whisked off the cloche. The lid was filled with steam – for a moment, Lewis thought that he was looking at a roast turkey. But as the steam cleared, he could see that it was no turkey: it was an enormous roasted bat, covered in scorched and smoking fur. Its blackened fangs were stretched wide open to reveal a writhing feast of spiders and fish eggs and scorpions inside, bubbling in its blood.

'My goodness – a Beelzebat!' said the Dean. 'I thought they were endangered?'

'Not any more,' said Wallmanner. 'Now they're extinct!'

He whipped a knife from his pocket and plunged it deep into the bat's skull.

'The Beelzebat is found only in the darkest rainforests of Southern America: locals always considered it the incarnation of the Devil himself. It is the perfect accompaniment for my tale – about a relative of mine who made a deal with the wrong man. His story, and his terrible fate, has been passed down through my family for generations . . .'

Bad Uncle Mortimer

Mortimer was a clever young man – the apple of his parents' eyes. But when he was sent to attend university in the city, he began to sour like a bad fruit. He fell in with a rough crowd and stopped going to classes. Soon he was spending his days at the dog track, gambling away his parents' money. When *that* was gone, he started borrowing from the local gangsters – in fact, he borrowed so much that soon he was heavily in debt.

Mortimer was too proud to beg his parents for more help – so instead, one fateful Christmas Eve, he borrowed money from every gangster in town and bet it all on one greyhound. The dog got scurvy halfway through the race and died. Mortimer was done for. Soon every hoodlum in the city was going to be knocking at his door, demanding money he didn't have.

So he did the only sensible thing a man in his position could do: he locked himself inside his library, sank into an armchair with a shotgun, and put his head in his hands.

'I'm doomed!' Mortimer cried. 'Oh, what I wouldn't give for another chance.'

'Perhaps I can be of help,' said a voice.

Mortimer leapt to his feet. He thought he was alone, but there was a man sitting in an armchair behind him. Mortimer was confused – he didn't even *own* another chair.

And yet there was the man, sitting in the shadows and helping himself to Mortimer's whisky like the two of them had been friends for years.

'Who are you? How did you get in here?'

The man laughed. 'That's no way to talk to a guest on Christmas Eve, Mortimer!'

Mortimer blinked. 'How do you know my name?'

'Everyone knows *you*, Mortimer!' said the man cheerily. 'Come, have a drink with me.'

Mortimer sat down, baffled. He had no idea how this man had managed to get inside his house – all the doors were locked. Mortimer couldn't even see what the man looked like – but he was filled with a terrible sense of dread in his presence. It crept up his legs like he'd stepped on a nest of spiders.

'Poor old Mortimer,' said the man. 'You're in a fine old mess, aren't you? Up to your eyeballs in debt, without a penny left to pay those gangsters!'

Mortimer had forgotten about his problems for a moment, but now they came flooding back. 'What can I do? Those gangsters will send my body to my mother in pieces!'

'What a Christmas present *that* would be!' sighed the man, shaking his head. 'You're lucky I came when I did. As it so happens, I'm in the business of helping those in need.'

The man leaned out of the shadows to refill his glass. Mortimer could see him now, clear as day. He wore an elegant suit, with a silk tie and a pair of polished brogues – but the man had no head. Instead, where the collar ended, there was nothing but a pillar of white smoke pouring out of his shirt like a chimney. The man took a sip of whisky and placed the glass beside him. A mouthful of smoke was left floating on the surface like a cloud.

'Are you ... the Devil?' Mortimer asked, terrified.

The Devil laughed. 'They were right about you, Mortimer – you're a smart lad! And a smart lad like you deserves some help when he's down on his luck.'

He held out his hands. They were as wide and as white as polished plates, piled high with gold coins. Mortimer's eyes sparkled just looking at them. There was more money than he needed – much more. Enough to pay off all his debts *and* live like a king afterwards.

'All you have to do is ask,' said the Devil.

Mortimer glanced up. 'What's the catch?'

The Devil leaned back. 'There is no catch. I'll give you all the money you need, and I ask for nothing in return.'

'Don't you want my soul?' said Mortimer. 'You *are* the Devil, aren't you?'

The Devil gave him a look that suggested

he was raising his eyebrows behind the white smoke.

'Mortimer – why would I expect an intelligent man like you to exchange his *immortal soul* for a handful of gold?'

Mortimer took a good, long look at the Devil. The Prince of Darkness wasn't anything like he'd expected. He'd always been told the Devil was a monster – but instead, he was friendly, well dressed and polite. Perhaps, thought Mortimer, I've been wrong about the Devil all along.

'You really want *nothing* in return?' he asked.

The Devil nodded, wafting the smoke into billowing waves.

'Fine,' said Mortimer. 'I'll take your offer. Leave me all the money I need and go.'

The Devil smiled. 'Your choice, Mortimer.'

And just like that, Mortimer woke up.

He had fallen asleep in his armchair; the bottle of whisky was empty beside him. He gazed around the library, and let out a nervous laugh.

'It . . . it was all a dream! Of course – how could I be so stupid? Everyone *knows* there's no such thing as the D—'

Mortimer trailed off. The library was filled from floor to ceiling with money – piles and piles of it. All of his furniture had been replaced by sacks of gold; all his books had been replaced by shelves of banknotes.

The armchair where the Devil had been sitting was still there. Tattooed into the fabric was the scorched outline of a man, sizzling in the darkness.

Someone hammered at the door.

'Mortimer – open up! We know you're in there! We just want to have a quiet, reasonable chat with you.'

Mortimer recognised the voice at once – it was Face-Smasher O'Sullivan, the most violent gangster in the city. Mortimer opened the door, and sure enough a patient queue of hoodlums was waiting outside with clubs and chains and bricks. Before any of them could strike the first blow, Mortimer handed each of them a bag of gold.

'There you go, gentlemen!' he said. 'Everything I owe, plus interest. Merry Christmas.'

The gangsters left, puzzled and slightly disappointed. Just like that, Mortimer was debt-free – and he had barely even scratched the surface of his new wealth.

Mortimer had been due to spend Christmas morning with his family, but he didn't much see the point in doing *that* any more. Instead, he filled a suitcase with money and set out for the poshest street in the city. It was a row of glorious mansion houses, each one more beautiful than the last. Mortimer knocked on the first door and a woman answered. She was wearing a nightgown and looked extremely irritated.

'Sorry to bother you,' said Mortimer. 'I'd like to buy your house.'

He held out a stack of banknotes a foot tall. The woman's eyes boggled – but she shook her head.

'Are you out of your mind? It's Christmas morning! My children are opening their presents! I'm not going to kick them out in the middle of the street just because—'

Mortimer doubled the stack of money in his hand.

'Give me ten minutes,' said the woman.

In less than five, her children were standing on the pavement bawling their eyes out, and Mortimer was the new owner of their house.

He didn't stop there – he bought every house on the street, until the pavements were covered in weeping children. He smashed through all the walls connecting them so that his mansion stretched from one end of the street to the other. It was the biggest house in the city – and it was all his.

Mortimer ordered a fleet of horse-drawn carriages to carry all the money from his library, and started to live like a king.

The next year passed in a blur. Mortimer was the richest man in the city – he wore the finest clothes, ate in the finest restaurants, and wore so much gold jewellery that he started to get backache from carrying it around all the time. Money left his hands in a constant stream – there seemed to be no end to his newfound wealth.

But of course, there *was* an end to it. In

twelve short months, his money dried up. It seemed to happen in an instant – one moment he was loaded, the next he was penniless. But it was even worse than that. On days when Mortimer had forgotten to bring his wallet – which happened often – he'd ask bars, casinos, restaurants and dog tracks to loan him money instead. They were only too happy to oblige – after all, Mortimer was the richest man in town. But now he was broke – again – and he owed thousands of pounds. *Hundreds* of thousands, in fact. He was in more debt than ever before.

So it was that the following Christmas Eve, Mortimer found himself slumped in another armchair in another library, cradling another shotgun. Of course, *this* armchair was plusher, and the library was bigger, and the shotgun fired diamonds instead of bullets.

'What have I done?' cried Mortimer. 'I

should have confessed to my family when I had the chance – I haven't even *seen* them in a year! Now I'm really done for!'

'Perhaps I can be of help,' said a voice.

Mortimer turned round. The Devil was once again sitting in an armchair behind him, drinking whisky. But Mortimer couldn't help noticing that the Devil looked different this time. He was taller – twice Mortimer's height, in fact. He towered over the chair he sat in like a hawk in a sparrow's nest. The smoke that billowed from his collar was darker than before.

'Oh, Devil!' cried Mortimer. 'You have to help me – the money you gave me wasn't enough! I need more!'

'Why didn't you ask sooner, Mortimer?' said the Devil. 'That can be easily fixed.'

Mortimer gulped. 'But . . . will it be the same deal this time? You don't want my soul?'

'I only want to *help*, Mortimer,' said the Devil kindly.

Mortimer breathed a sigh of relief.

'Good! Then fill up this library with money again – and this time, give me all I'll ever need so I can never run out!'

The Devil nodded, rippling the black smoke.

'Your choice, Mortimer.'

And just like that, Mortimer woke up. He couldn't believe his eyes. The vast library was packed with gold and jewellery, right up to the rafters. He had never seen so much money in his life – a hundred men living a hundred lifetimes could never *hope* to spend it.

So Mortimer decided to try.

He stopped going out to fancy restaurants – instead, he bought every chef in the city and paid for them to live in his house. Each evening, they'd present him with a variety of meals – Mortimer would choose one he wanted and throw the other two hundred away. Instead of spending his nights at dog tracks and casinos, Mortimer had his own dog track and casino installed in the mansion, complete with hundreds of people paid an hourly wage to stand around looking like they were having a good time. Mortimer installed his own cinemas, ice rinks, fairgrounds and theatres right beside him, and when he ran out of space, Mortimer simply bought every house in the next street and smashed through the walls.

As Mortimer's house grew bigger, so too did Mortimer. All that fine dining made him enormous, and within a few months he was so fat that he couldn't walk around his mansion any more – instead, he sat on his pile of gold like a sultan and made people come to him. He'd throw money when he liked them, and throw money *at* them when he was bored.

Soon, another Christmas arrived. Mortimer was celebrating this one in style, eating a whole roast goose by himself while thousands of hired guests cheered and praised him.

'Mortimer's the best!'

'Three cheers for Mortimer!'

'Have you lost weight, Mortimer?'

Mortimer took another huge bite of goose – and choked. His eyes grew wide, and his face turned bright red. He tumbled from the pile of money and collapsed on the floor, clutching at his chest.

'Hey! What's wrong with old fatty?' said one of his guests.

'He's having a heart attack!' said another. 'What do we do?'

'Quick!' said the first one. 'Grab as much money as you can before he dies!'

Mortimer's fake friends piled wads of cash into their pockets and scattered from the house like rats, leaving him to perish on the floor. Mortimer lay alone, gasping his final breaths in the empty room.

'Please!' he cried. 'Someone! *Anyone!*'

'Perhaps I can be of help,' said a voice.

Mortimer looked up, his face dripping with sweat. On the other side of the enormous room sat the Devil, back in his old armchair – but once again, he looked different. The chair had become red-hot embers where he touched it. The smoke that poured out of his collar was now deepest black, filling the room like a volcano.

'Devil!' cried Mortimer. 'Oh, you have to help me – I'm dying!'

'I can see that, Mortimer,' said the Devil. 'How much money would you like this time?'

Mortimer shook his head. 'No! I don't want any more money – I want *life*!'

The Devil shook his head. 'I'm afraid I can't do that, Mortimer. It's your time to go.'

Mortimer's eyes widened with horror.

'Please – I just want another day! Enough to see my family again and ask for their forgiveness! I'll give you whatever you want – anything!'

The Devil chuckled. 'And what do you have that I might *possibly* want, Mortimer?'

Mortimer swallowed hard. He knew the answer.

'I . . . I'll give you my immortal soul!'

The Devil paused. 'Your *soul*, you say?'

Mortimer nodded. 'Yes – it's all yours! Just don't let me die!'

The Devil gave a deep sigh, and stood up from the armchair. He made his way across the room towards Mortimer, growing taller and taller with every step. The smoke that billowed from his neck grew blacker and thicker, pouring up into the ceiling like a waterfall; his elegant suit burned to ashes. The lights in the room went out one by one as he passed them.

'I'm afraid that won't do, Mortimer,' said the Devil, his voice growing louder and louder. 'You see – your soul is mine already. You gave it to me a long time ago.'

Mortimer gasped. 'No . . . We had a deal! You said the money was free! You said you weren't going to take my soul!'

The Devil laughed. 'Clever boy, aren't you Mortimer? I never *took* your soul – you gave it to me willingly.'

The Devil stood over him. Mortimer could see his entire body was covered in thick, coarse hair, and his bright white hands had sharpened into terrible claws. He was so tall that his smoking head touched the ceiling.

'I gave you more money than you ever needed. Did you give it to those that did? No.

Did you use it to make a difference to the world? NO. Did you return to your family, who gave you everything they had? NO! You used the money to turn yourself into a bully, a sloth and a tyrant. I didn't have to do a thing, Mortimer – you handed me your soul on a platter!'

The Devil crouched down low, until Mortimer's face stung and sizzled with the heat that roared off him. Mortimer tried to turn away, but it was too late – he was dying. When the Devil next spoke, his voice was as loud as a thunderstorm.

'It was your choice, Mortimer. And you chose Hell.'

The smoke parted, and with his dying breath Mortimer finally saw the Devil's face that had lain hidden behind the smoke all this time.

It was his own, staring back at him.

The guests howled with delight once more. Lewis stood at the edge of the room, his heart pounding. He couldn't believe how happy these people were to hear such horrible stories – the more unpleasant the tale, the happier they seemed.

'Great stuff, Wallmanner!' said the Dean. 'A classic tale with a family connection – that's sure *to win you some extra points!'*

Lady Arabella shifted angrily in her chair.

'Pah! My story was ten times *better than that piece of claptrap!'*

Wallmanner shot her a furious look. 'No one cares what you think, you fat old hag!'

Before Lady Arabella could respond, Wallmanner had already leapt onto the table and kicked a whole jug of gravy over her. Lady Arabella shrieked – on cue, her dogs flew at the guests, snapping at their ankles. Within seconds the whole table was at each other's throats, clawing and biting one another.

Lewis was stunned. The guests had turned on each other in an instant – only the Dean stayed in his chair, staring at them in shock. He leapt to his feet.

'STOP!'

The fighting stopped instantly.

'YOU KNOW THE RULES!' *bellowed the Dean. 'The best story is decided at the end of the night! We stick to the rules laid down by Edgar Caverner, or we fall apart. We're here to destroy Christmas – not each other!'*

The guests muttered in agreement and returned sheepishly to their chairs. The Dean glared at Retch and Lady Arabella with a look that could burn through glass.

'Now, spit and make up.'

The two guests reluctantly spat on each other and sat back down. Was that an apology? *Lewis was disgusted.*

But at the same time, he was hatching a plan. A plan to escape from the College alive.

'Now let's get back to what really matters – our night of stories!' The Dean lifted the next bauble and smashed it on the table. 'Our next tale is from Sir Algernon Thoroughbred-Pilt, High Master of Flogging!'

The clock struck two, and the kitchen doors swung open. Balanced in the Cook's hands was a giant gingerbread house, decorated with icing and lollipops and hard candy windowpanes. Lewis grabbed it and placed it on the table before anyone could take a swipe at his head.

'A gingerbread house?' *said the Dean, unimpressed. 'Care to explain yourself, Pilt? This is a Dinner of Souls, not a children's tea party!'*

The man in the filthy pinstripe suit and broken bowler hat stood up. He was covered from head to toe in heavy gold chains: one hung from the monocle jammed in his eye, and a dozen more swung from his pockets. There was even one attached to the club he carried in his belt.

'A *house's* exterior *can never be trusted, Dean,' Sir Algernon Thoroughbred-Pilt said calmly. 'Remember that a wall can hide a great many evils. People so rarely choose to look beyond them.'*

He removed the front of the gingerbread house, revealing the scene inside. The guests gasped: it was a gingerbread torture chamber, with a pastry executioner wielding a sharpened candy cane. In front of him a helpless jelly baby victim dangled over a cauldron of hot chocolate sauce.

'This is no dusty family story,' *announced Sir Algernon, shooting a glance at Retch Wallmanner. 'This happened to a close friend of mine, one Christmas Eve not so long ago. I tell it to you exactly as he told it to me . . .'*

He plucked the gingerbread executioner out of the house and chewed on its head thoughtfully as he told his grisly tale.

The Kensington System

I was driving to my aunt's house one Christmas Eve when my car broke down. The timing couldn't have been worse – I was alone, in the middle of nowhere, and it was already dark. Snow was falling so heavily that I could barely see ten feet ahead of me. I wandered down the road, shivering as I searched for any sign of life – and to my relief, found a set of iron gates.

They led to a mansion – a mansion that,

even through the snow and darkness, I could see was brutally ugly. It may have *once* been beautiful, but over time something had warped it. Still, I had little choice: the snow was getting heavier every second. I raced to the door and rang the bell.

It was some time before the door opened. When it did, I was confronted by an old man – at least, I *think* he was old. He looked like wet newspaper left out to dry on a skeleton.

'Can I help you?' he said, his voice no more than a croak.

I smiled nervously. 'My car broke down outside. I was wondering if I could use your phone to—'

'The nearest phone is in town,' he said. 'Ten miles away. Your best bet is to walk there in the morning when the storm has passed.'

My face fell. 'Tomorrow? But it's Christmas Eve! My aunt—'

'It would be a pleasure to have you, sir,' said the man, leading me inside. 'We rarely have guests nowadays at Kensington Manor.'

I could see why – the house was even more miserable on the inside. The walls were covered in dust and the carpet disintegrated beneath my feet. But the worst part of all was the *feeling* in the house. It was like something terrible had happened there a long time ago – something which still hadn't left.

'My name is Jasper,' said the man. 'I look after Kensington Manor by myself nowadays. I can tell you all about its rich history tomorrow morning!'

The last thing I wanted to do was spend Christmas Eve in that horrible house – but there was no point in refusing. Besides, I could always get up early and leave before Jasper woke up – I'd be at my aunt's in time for Christmas breakfast.

Jasper led me to my bedroom, a tiny box with four walls, no windows, and an old damp bed.

'The master suite,' he said grandly. 'You'll be quite comfortable here, sir. Scream if you need anything.'

'I'm sure I'll be fine,' I said.

Jasper showed me his teeth. It took me a while before I realised he was smiling.

'I'm sure,' he said, and closed the door.

I gazed at the dismal room and shuddered. A prison cell would have been cosier. For a brief moment, I even considered going back outside to spend the night in my car – then I remembered how cold it was.

'Just go to sleep,' I muttered to myself. 'You'll be out of here soon.'

I clambered into my damp bed, turned off the lights, and waited for sleep to come.

*

The sound woke me at midnight.

I sat bolt upright. My room was pitch black. I couldn't see my own hand in front of my face. Outside, the storm was raging at the windowpanes – but I could hear another sound beneath it.

Scrape, scrape, scrape.

It was coming from the wall behind me.

I flew out of the bed. I wasn't imagining it: there was something scratching at my bedroom wall. But this was no trapped rat in the wall space. I was listening to the slow, desperate scrape of human fingernails. I could even track them as they moved in the darkness – *scrape, scrape, scrape*, from one side of the room to the other . . .

And that wasn't all I could hear. There was a voice, too.

'Please . . . please . . .'

I stood stock-still, my heart pounding. The

scraping moved down the hallway, growing quieter and quieter. Then it simply faded into silence.

I didn't dare move – I barely dared to breathe. I knew what I had heard – there was someone trapped in the walls of Kensington Manor.

But how was that possible . . . ?

When I finally felt brave enough to move, I turned on my bedside lamp and dressed frantically. It was no good – I wasn't going to spend another second in that awful house. I turned to grab my bag—

And stopped. There was something on the table beside me – something I hadn't noticed earlier. A book, its cover as dark and grim as the wood it rested on. The front read:

The Secret Diary of Eliza Kensington

I don't know why I did it. I don't know why I didn't just run. But something deep down told me that the book was important. Something told me that this would explain everything: this would reveal the secret of the scraping in the walls. I picked up the book and opened its brown, curling pages. Inside was line after line of frantic, spidery handwriting:

If you are reading this diary, then know two things: my name is Eliza Kensington, and I am being kept prisoner in my own house.

My heart raced. It was the hidden diary of a young girl, written almost a hundred years ago.

I do not know what is going to happen to me, but a terrible crime is being committed here at Kensington

Manor. If I do not leave this note, then maybe my terrible fate will never be discovered – maybe all my suffering will be for nothing!

I couldn't believe what I was reading. I sat down on the bed and read on as the terrible story unfolded before me.

I was born Eliza Kensington. My mother and father were Lord and Lady Kensington: they adored me, and I adored them. I have never known two people more kind or loving. All my parents ever wanted was that I should be happy, no matter what path in life I chose.

Then one week ago . . . my world ended.

My parents were on a trip when

their ship was hit by a terrible storm. Every passenger on board perished, and at a mere twelve years old I was left an orphan. I have no brothers or sisters to look after me – all my father's relatives are long dead. My mother spoke once of some far-off cousins whom she had never met, but no one has been able to trace them.

So I have been handed over to the two most despicable fiends to ever walk the earth – Mr Boggs and Mr Ulcer!

They are half-step-godsons of my father's maiden aunt's cousin, twice removed: the only living relatives that my family lawyers could find. They both arrived at Kensington Manor this morning, stinking of tobacco and bacon. Neither of them were wearing socks.

It's impossible to decide which of the two men is worse. Boggs is slovenly and unwashed, as squat as a fistful of mince; Ulcer is a bony weasel with cruel yellow eyes and a pudding-bowl haircut. He is the 'brains' of the operation, which isn't saying much.

'So! This is the girl, is it?' said Boggs, leering at me with beery breath. 'The little runt we're expected to look after, without ever seeing a penny for our troubles?'

I was shocked – was this the first thing my new guardians would say to a young girl who had just lost both her parents? But mother and father always taught me to be polite to others, no matter how disgusting, so I gave them my warmest smile.

'Hello, Uncles,' I said. 'It's a pleasure to—'

'Put a sock in it, squirt!' snapped Ulcer. 'Let's get this straight, right here and now – we don't want to be here! Thanks to you, our carefree bachelor days are over, so you'd better start making it up to us, fast!'

I couldn't believe my ears – these two spoiled, lazy rats wanted nothing to do with me!

'Well in that case,' I said, 'you can leave. I'm sorry to have taken up your time.'

Boggs and Ulcer shared a look – and laughed.

'Oh, we're not going anywhere, girl!' said Boggs. 'We're your guardians – that means that until you're eighteen years old, you're our property! Your idiot parents might not have left us a penny, but there are other ways we can make money off of you . . .'

'That's right!' said Ulcer. 'We have great plans for you, my girl. Great plans indeed!'

With that, the two men threw me into my bedroom and locked the door. I can hear them downstairs now, drinking their way through my parents' wine cellar and shouting at the servants!

I have no idea what terrible fate awaits me. Will those two awful men put me in the workhouse? Cut off all my hair and sell it to wigmakers? Force me to be their slave?

No matter what happens, I must remember that I am a Kensington. We are strong; we cannot be broken by anyone!

Day 1

Boggs and Ulcer kicked down my door this morning and dragged me out of bed.

'Downstairs, runt!' cried Boggs. 'Your lessons start now!'

I was confused. 'Lessons? But it's a Sunday – my science and maths tutors don't arrive until tomorrow—'

'Science? Maths?' spat Boggs. 'Pah! You can forget all that rubbish! From now on, you'll be studying nothing but the Kensington System!'

I had never heard of the Kensington System – no one has. Boggs and Ulcer invented it while drunk last night. Boggs had wanted to call it the Boggs System, Ulcer had wanted to call it the Ulcer System. In the end they reached a compromise.

'A pretty little girl like you has no use for books,' Ulcer explained. 'It's time you were made a lady – a proper one! The kind a rich prince would want to marry!'

'That's right.' Boggs giggled. 'And pay us a handsome sum for the privilege, too!'

I finally understood Boggs's and Ulcer's terrible plan: they were going to wait until I was old enough to marry and then sell me off to some foreign prince like a farmyard animal! I glared at them defiantly.

'I refuse – I don't want to be a princess!'

'Tough!' said Boggs. 'We're your guardians, and we're going to train you in the Kensington System whether you like it or not!'

'Starting with these filthy clothes,' said Ulcer, tugging at my dress. 'First rule of the Kensington System: only perfection is allowed!'

From now on, I am to wear ball gowns and a full face of make-up – from first thing in the morning to last thing at night! I kicked and fought against Boggs and Ulcer with all my might, but it was no use. They wrapped me in bodices that stabbed and pinched my sides, and strapped my feet in high-heel shoes that burn my ankles and make my toes sing with pain. Then they made me watch as they burned all my clothes in a bonfire in the middle of the dining room.

'That's enough lessons for today!' cried Ulcer. 'Back to your room!'

They left me alone in the dark of my bedroom once again; only now my body is so racked with pain I can barely move, let alone sleep!

Oh diary, what could they possibly have in store for me tomorrow?

Day 2

When Boggs and Ulcer led me downstairs this morning, I was

shocked at the state of the house. All the windows have been barred; all the doors have been locked.

'What have you done?' I cried. 'How will I ever get outside?'

'You don't <u>need</u> to go outside!' snapped Boggs. 'Second rule of the Kensington System: a princess's home is her castle!'

From now on, I will be shut inside Kensington Manor from dawn to dusk. I am to be kept a prisoner in my own home until the day I'm married!

'You can't do this!' I cried. 'When my friends find out—'

'From now on, you don't have any friends!' Ulcer cackled. 'Rule number three: a perfect lady must be left alone!'

From now on, I am forbidden

from speaking to anyone other than Boggs and Ulcer – and that includes the servants. If any of them talk to me – or are even seen in the same room as me – they will be sacked on the spot. Boggs and Ulcer have even installed hundreds of mirrors on every wall of the house so that the servants can see me coming at all times.

Well, that was the final straw. My parents always raised me to speak my mind, and as long as I carry their spirit in my heart, I will fight for what is right! I stamped my feet with fury.

'You awful brutes. I won't stand for it. Get out of my house at once, or I'll make you regret the day you ever crossed a Kensington!'

Boggs laughed. 'We're your guardians, you stupid girl – until you're eighteen, you have to do everything we say! And don't forget the most important rule of the Kensington System: Silence – Is – Golden!'

Oh diary, this is the most fiendish rule of them all. From now on, I will be banned from talking! If I speak – if I make so much as a peep – I'm to be punished. A word out of place, a hummed tune, a cry of pain when I fall over – they're all forbidden!

I seethed. 'You can punish me all you like – I won't let you win! I'll fight you with everything I have!'

Boggs and Ulcer were furious – they whipped me till I bled and locked me in my bedroom.

'Let that be a lesson to you!' snapped Ulcer through the keyhole. 'You need to learn some manners if you want to bag a prince!'

Their cackles echoed down the corridor as they ran off.

Oh diary, my body is in even more agony than before. But I must be brave. I must keep fighting! If not, what kind of future awaits me in Kensington Manor? To spend my days sitting in mute silence in the darkness, caked in make-up like a china doll?

Mother, Father, give me the strength to beat them. I cannot let them win. I cannot!

<u>Day 3</u>

My war against Boggs and Ulcer

has begun.

This morning I broke all the mirrors in the house, smashed down the back doors and threw all my ballgowns in the lake. Boggs and Ulcer caught me, of course, and dragged me kicking and screaming back to Kensington Manor. I got another whipping for my defiance – and then they took down every portrait of my mother and father they could find and tore them to pieces in front of me.

I wept furious tears. Some of the servants – the ones I have lived with and loved since I was a baby – tried to stop them, but of course they were sacked on the spot.

My heart aches with sadness – but I cannot stop now, diary. I cannot let them win – I must keep going!

Day 4

Today I did everything in my power to break the rules of the Kensington System. I ran through the house screaming at the top of my lungs. I smashed every window. I stamped my make-up into paste. Boggs and Ulcer punished me over and over and over. They took away my bed: they stopped feeding me. Thank goodness I had safely hidden this diary – if they ever find out about its existence, who knows what they would do to me!

I can hear them downstairs now, trying to come up with some other fiendish punishment to break me – but they will all fail. After all, I am a Kensington! And as long as I have my parents' love in my heart, there is <u>nothing</u> they can do that will break me! Nothing!

Day 10

Oh diary, how wrong I was.

My hand is shaking as I write this. Five days ago Boggs and Ulcer dragged me from my bedroom – but this time, they were smiling.

'Quite the handful, aren't you?' said Ulcer. 'We've had a hard job thinking up a good punishment for you – but this time, we think we might have struck gold!' He turned to his accomplice. 'Tell me, Boggs – what frightens people more than anything?'

'Goldfish!' Boggs cried.

'No, you idiot,' said Ulcer. 'Being alone! Trapped in darkness! Feeling like you might scream and scream, and no one will ever hear you!'

My heart froze. They were leading me down a long corridor. At the far end, a hole was ripped in the wall. Inside was purest darkness.

'We discovered a little secret about Kensington Manor,' said Ulcer. 'There's a space between the walls that runs from one end of the house to the other. It's just big enough for a person to squeeze through – but only just. It's cramped and dark and full of spiders and the floor is thick with the bones of filthy rats!'

The two men thrust me into the darkness.

'This is where you live from now on,' said Boggs. 'That is, until you learn to behave yourself!'

'We'll start you off with a taster,' said Ulcer. 'Five days! Don't worry, there's plenty of insects to eat if you get hungry!'

I cried out and fought against them – but it was no use. The two men were too strong for me. They heaved a wardrobe in front of the hole and closed up the wall.

Oh diary – how can I describe what it's like in there? The space between the walls seems to stretch on forever – but there's not even enough room to turn around.
As you drag yourself along, the walls crush you and rub your skin raw, splintering your hands to bleeding. Rats scuttle over your feet and spiders cover your face.

The dust chokes you and burns your eyes – oh, how it burns!

But worst of all is the darkness. It seems to go on forever – you can scream and scream into it and pound the walls, but no one ever hears. No one comes to help. All you can do is walk the walls, searching for any hope of escape . . . but of course, there is none.

After five days and five nights in hell, Boggs and Ulcer let me out and flung me back into my room. I wept for hours. Oh, thank goodness for this diary – thank goodness I have some way to tell the world what these monsters are doing to me! My only hope is that by keeping a record of it all, it will one day lead to their arrest. I shall write down every cruelty they commit!

The thought of going back into the walls is terrifying – but I must be brave. I must not let them break me. I must keep fighting, with all my heart!

If not, then ... oh diary, what will become of me?

I lowered the book in horror. I struggled to make sense of what I'd read. How could two men lock a twelve-year-old girl in the walls? Was that really what I had just heard, scraping above my head?

But it couldn't be – Eliza Kensington had written her diary almost a hundred years ago. She would be dead by now. There was no *way* she could still be crying and scratching inside the walls.

Unless ...

No. I refused to believe in ghosts. There had to be some other, more rational explanation. Surely Eliza had escaped the house – surely she had been saved, and her dreadful tormentors locked up for their crimes?

But the more I flicked through the diary, the more I realised that it wasn't true. The handwriting became more erratic, the sentences more confused. Days would go past without any writing at all – sometimes weeks. Eliza's spidery handwriting became even smaller as she tried to fit in her increasingly rambling sentences.

Then, I found it: her final entry. It was crushed into the corner of the last page of the diary, the ink smudged and blotting:

Day 1,432

Darkness. That is all I know now.

Boggs and Ulcer are winning, diary.
I am going mad.

I cannot spend another second in those walls – I cannot feel my fingers bleed against the wood one moment longer. I cannot eat any more insects to survive. I cannot fight them any more – I am done. They have broken me.

There is no escape from Kensington Manor. I must become the princess they want me to be, or else I will go mad. My only hope is that one day someone will discover this diary and know what happened – that I will not have suffered all this in vain.

Oh, Mother, Father ... forgive me!

'You screamed, sir?'

I yelped with fright. Jasper was standing in the doorway.

'Sorry I took so long,' he said. 'I was boiling some eggs for Christmas dinner.'

He held up a large bowl filled with a hundred hard-boiled eggs.

'Jasper.' I was trembling – I must have been white as a sheet. 'What on earth . . .'

'Egg, sir?'

Jasper offered me the bowl. I shook my head. He sat down beside me.

'I do apologise about the noise, sir. It can be a terrible effort sleeping at Kensington Manor sometimes with all that scratching and wailing. This was once the most beautiful stately home in the country – but no one cares to visit any more. The noises put people off – that and its tragic history. Memories like that have a tendency to stain a place.'

My eyes widened. 'You mean . . . Eliza

Kensington?'

Jasper carefully severed off the top of an egg with a practised movement.

'I see you found her diary. It's a terrible shame, what those men did to her. Boggs and Ulcer started locking Eliza in the walls for weeks at a time. She'd wander from one end of the house to the other, scratching at the walls and sobbing. Enough to drive anyone mad. Soon enough, the Kensington System began to work – Eliza stopped fighting back. She stopped talking. Finally, she stopped thinking. She'd spend whole days sitting in a chair like a china doll, blinking silently in the darkness.'

I stared at Jasper, completely aghast. I tried to find the right words.

'Jasper . . . are you trying to tell me that I've been listening to the ghost of a twelve-year-old girl who was *tortured to death in this house*?'

Jasper stared at me for a moment – then laughed.

'Forgive me, sir – I keep forgetting how little you know of Kensington Manor! I'm guessing you haven't heard what happened to Eliza when she turned eighteen years old?'

I shook my head. Jasper smiled.

'You see, as Eliza got older, news of a beautiful young lady at Kensington Manor spread across the world. Boggs and Ulcer waited expectantly for the offers to come rolling in and, sure enough, on the morning of her eighteenth birthday, they heard a knock at the door. When they opened it, a royal regiment strode inside. They were all wearing the coat of arms of Lutgenstein – the wealthiest royal family in the world!

'"Good afternoon, gentlemen," said the messenger. "I have come to seek out the young Lady Eliza."

'Eliza sat serene and blank in the corner. She had barely even noticed the men walk in.

'"There she is!" cried Ulcer. "One hundred per cent bona fide princess material!" He rubbed his hands with glee. "Where is he then? Where's the lucky Prince of Lutgenstein?"

'"Dead, sir," said the messenger.

'The uncles were confused. "Dead?"

'"Along with the King and Queen," said the messenger. "And all their children. The entire Lutgenstein royal family was wiped out last year in our country's worst-ever Zeppelin accident. First cousins, second cousins, great aunts, grandnephews ... every single one of them, incinerated! We've spent *months* searching for a last living Lutgenstein."

'The uncles were furious.

'"Well, what are you wasting our time for?" said Boggs. "We can't marry Eliza to a dead prince!"

'The messenger smiled.

'"We're not here to discuss marriage, gentlemen. We're here because this lady's mother" – he pointed to Eliza – "was the last remaining Lutgenstein. Which makes Eliza the rightful heir to the family throne!"

'The entire regiment bowed down to Eliza. Boggs and Ulcer could hardly contain their delight. They leapt and danced around the room.

'"We did it, Boggs!" Ulcer cried. "What a prize we bagged – queen of the wealthiest royal family in the world! We're rich beyond our wildest dreams . . ."

'"Are you now?"

'The uncles spun round. To their surprise, Eliza had stood up. Her eyes – which had been blank for so many years – had flickered back to life.

'"Sit down and shut up, girl!" said Boggs. "We're your guardians, and—"

'"Not any more," said Eliza. "I'm eighteen years old today – which means from now on, I make my own decisions. And I will see that you two despicable men never get a single penny."

'Eliza's spirit hadn't gone at all – it had simply learned how to hide. It had learned to protect itself. It had found a place in her heart where no one else could ever find it – where her parents' love had always stayed with her – and it had waited for the right moment to come back out.

'Ulcer stormed forward, his hand raised to strike. "Why, you ungrateful little—!"

'In an instant there were ten swords at his throat.

'"How *dare* you threaten the Queen of Lutgenstein!" cried the messenger. "Men have been cut to pieces for less!"

'Boggs and Ulcer looked round with

panicked eyes. They were surrounded by soldiers – and standing behind them was Eliza, her eyes shining like daggers.

'"What shall we do with them, Your Majesty?" asked the messenger. "Cut their throats? Feed them to the dogs? Whip their skin off, inch by inch?"

'Eliza looked at the two men who had tortured her beyond imagining – and for the first time in six years, a smile came to the corner of her lips.

'"No," she said. "I have a much better idea."

'The soldiers took Boggs and Ulcer upstairs and pushed them into the walls of Kensington Manor. They covered the entrance up with cement, locked the mansion behind them, and left forever. Boggs and Ulcer hammered at the walls, and kicked and howled and begged for mercy, but there was no one to hear them.

'Eliza ruled as Queen of Lutgenstein for many, many years – in fact, she's considered the most beloved monarch in their entire history. And funnily enough, she never did get married. Strange how life pans out, isn't it?'

Jasper finished his story with a smile, and calmly ate his egg. I stared at him with horror.

'So . . . those noises,' I whispered. 'Those desperate, wretched cries in the walls – the scraping of fingers above my head – I was listening to the ghosts of . . . *Boggs and Ulcer?*'

Jasper stopped, an egg halfway to his mouth. He turned to me with a frown.

' . . . Who said anything about them being dead?'

The story finished, and the guests gave another shrieking round of applause.

'A marvellous story, Sir Algernon!' said the Dean. 'And what a novel treat – a gingerbread house of horrors!'

'Plus we ate dessert before the main course,' said a guest. 'Now that's really *naughty.'*

Meanwhile, Lewis ran round the table emptying out another two bottles of gin. He had a plan now – he knew exactly what he had to do. He had to get the guests drunk. The more drunk they were, the more likely they were to start fighting again – then he might finally have a chance to sneak outside and warn someone about what was going on.

Three stories so far, *Lewis whispered to himself.* That means I have four stories to make sure they're all steaming drunk, or else . . .

He went to refill the Dean's glass – and stopped.

It was full to the brim – still untouched from his first toast. The Dean hadn't drunk a single drop all night.

The Dean's arm shot out and struck the glass from the table. It flew across the room and shattered on the far wall.

'You clumsy brat! Go and get the next course, before I poke your eyes out!'

Lewis was driven from the table in a barrage of jeers and flung cutlery. He stared at the Dean in confusion – that was no accident. The Dean had destroyed his glass on purpose, before Lewis could say anything.

But why . . . ?

The clock struck three, and the Cook lurched through the doors and handed the next course to Lewis. Lewis was surprised – this was no meal. It was a tray of ordinary Christmas crackers. The Dean smashed the next bauble and held up the piece of paper.

'Miss Ariadne Biter – Vice Chancellor of Poisoning!' He glared across the table. 'This is quite unorthodox, Miss Biter – where's your course?'

A woman stood at the end of the table – the one who had ridden a horse through the window earlier. She was still covered in cuts and scratches, and her face was sharp and twisted as a fossil.

'The course is inside *the cracker, Dean,' she explained. 'See for yourselves!'*

The Dean rolled his eyes, and passed the crackers around the table. The guests were clearly unimpressed – after all, they hated Christmas traditions. They held crackers with the people next to them as Ariadne Biter counted down.

'3-2-1-pull!'

KABOOM!

The explosion was deafening – loud enough to send Lewis flying backwards across the room. The few windows that were left unbroken shattered, and the guests were sent sprawling across the floor.

Lewis peered up blearily, his ears ringing. A heavy cloud of black smoke lingered over the room. A chandelier fell and smashed on the table.

The Dean sat up, his face blackened. 'Biter – you could have killed us all!' He nodded *approvingly. 'Bravo!'*

'Oh, I don't know if it could have killed *you, Dean,' Biter said bashfully. 'It was only a small, controlled explosion! Enough to blind you at worst.'*

The guests applauded politely and rejoined the

table as Ariadne Biter adjusted her smoking hair.

'Strange, isn't it? You expect one thing, and you get another. It happens all the time – for example, it might surprise you all to know that I was once a very nice girl! Of course, that was many years ago now – before I first heard of Soul's College, and came to follow the teachings of Edgar Caverner. Before that first fateful Christmas, when I learned that beneath the everyday world lurks a dark and secret place . . .'

Miss Magpie

My mother and I used to live on the poor side of the city. It was a different time then – families were often packed ten to a bedroom, and landlords were tyrants. If you couldn't pay the rent, they'd chuck you out onto the street without a second's thought.

My mother and I were lucky: our landlady was kind. She'd give tenants an extra week to gather their rent if they needed to. She even let one of the tenants live there for free: an old woman called Miss Magpie. That wasn't her real name, of course: everyone called her that because of the black-and-white dress she wore every single day. And, of course, because of her birds.

Miss Magpie lived on the same floor as us, at the very top of the building. She had the attic room to herself, up a spidery flight of steps behind a door she kept shut with ten locks. She lived by a strict routine, which – until that fateful Christmas – never once changed. Each morning, she'd lock the door behind her and head down the stairs in little pigeon steps, her ancient, wrinkled hands gripped tight on the banister. It would take her at least an hour to reach the bottom. Then she'd head across the road to the park and spend all day feeding the pigeons. When it got dark she'd come back inside, make her way up the creaking attic staircase with slow, trembling steps, and lock herself inside again.

No one knew why the landlady didn't charge her – in fact, no one knew *anything* about Miss Magpie. She was a complete mystery, like something out of time. No one ever saw her speak, no one ever saw her eat – she seemed to live only for her birds. I once joked to my mother that perhaps she was already dead – and my mother was furious.

'Never talk about the elderly like that! It can't be easy, being her age and having no family left to look after her. We could all end up like that one day!'

I wasn't so sure that Miss Magpie was just a harmless old lady. There were moments, when passing her on the stairs, that I'd suddenly catch her watching me with her beady black eyes. Her face would be cold and blank. It wasn't like a person was watching me: it was like being studied by an animal.

And of course, the fact she was 'just an old lady' still didn't answer the biggest mystery of all. What on earth did Miss Magpie do with herself on those long cold nights, alone in her attic room, without her precious birds?

Then one Christmas . . . I found out.

It was mid-December when it began. The shops were filled with Christmas displays and frantic shoppers, and the streets were hung with twinkling lights. Carollers stood on street corners and sang songs; the city felt special. I was sitting on the front steps of the building and reading a book. I was happy.

Then a pair of fake leather shoes appeared on the pavement in front of me and someone closed my book with the end of a long black cane.

'Where's your dad?'

It was a young man with a bad moustache: I hated him instantly. Every part of him was slick and false, from his shiny suit to his polished fingernails.

'I live with my mother,' I said.

'Then go get her!' he snapped. 'It's the end of the month – rent's due!'

I was confused. 'Where's the landlady?'

The man sniggered. 'Old cow carked it in the middle of the night. She's dead! Kicked the bucket! Which makes me, her beloved nephew, your new landlord!'

He barged past me and started pounding on every door.

'Open up! I want six months' rent in advance from everyone, right now!'

Six months rent! It was unthinkable – far more than anyone could afford, especially at Christmas. People begged for more time to find the money, but the landlord refused. Soon the road outside our building was covered in crying families with nowhere to go, clutching their few belongings.

We were lucky – my mother had been secretly saving up for months to buy me a Christmas present. She handed over the money with tears in her eyes, and the landlord stuffed it in his pocket without even bothering to count it.

'What about that room?' he grunted. 'Who lives in there?'

He nodded to Miss Magpie's door at the end of the corridor. My mother steeled herself.

'An old lady. Your aunt let her live here for free.'

The landlord's hat nearly popped off his head.

'*Free?* Am I hearing things?' He hammered on the door. 'Open up, you old bat! Your days of sponging off me are over – I want all the rent you owe, right now!'

Of course, Miss Magpie was still in the park – but we weren't going to tell him that. The landlord took a set of keys from his pocket and tried to unlock the bolts on the door. To his surprise, none of them worked.

'Fixing her own locks, is she? That's a criminal offence, that is! I could have her arrested!'

'Please, leave her alone,' my mother begged. 'She's a frail old lady – she'll never survive if you kick her out now!'

At that moment, as if by magic, Miss Magpie appeared at the top of the stairs. I was surprised to see her – she was hours earlier than usual. It was like she knew what was going on. The landlord stormed down the corridor and blocked her path.

'Ha! Thought you could lock me out, did

you? Well, I want all the rent you owe *and* compensation for that door!'

He trailed off. Miss Magpie hadn't even noticed him – she simply hobbled past, her eyes fixed to the floor as she made her way to the attic. The landlord was shocked for a moment – then his face turned nasty. He grabbed her by the arm, digging his polished fingernails deep into her flesh.

'Listen, you deaf old coot—'

Miss Magpie whipped round and thrashed him across the knees with her walking stick. The *crack* was agonising – the landlord howled with pain. Then, with incredible strength, Miss Magpie flipped him off his feet and sent him pinwheeling over the banister. The landlord tumbled down the stairs, hitting every step along the way before smashing into the Christmas tree at the bottom, dazed and groaning.

My mother and I were speechless. We never expected Miss Magpie to move so quickly – let alone have the strength to throw someone down the stairs. It was as though she was sixty years younger all of a sudden. We watched in amazement as she calmly unlocked her attic room, hobbled into her private world, and shut us out once more.

The landlord staggered to his feet on the floor below.

'That . . . that does it! You're out of here! You hear me? OUT!'

He stormed outside and disappeared. My mother was terrified for Miss Magpie. She knocked on her door and pleaded with her to listen, to come out before it was too late – but Miss Magpie stayed in her room, silent as always.

The landlord soon returned – and this time he had company: four equally greasy friends, all hair oil and pointy shoes. Each of them carried a sledgehammer. Before I knew what was happening, Mother had thrown me into our flat and shut me inside – all I could do was press my ear to the wall and listen as the landlord pounded on Miss Magpie's door and my mother tried to stop him.

'For heavens' sake, she's a harmless old lady! You should all be ashamed of yourselves!'

The landlord ignored her. 'One more chance, you foul old bat – open this door or we'll break it down and drag you out!'

There was no answer – the attic was as silent as ever. I heard the landlord step back.

'Right, lads, let her have it!'

The corridor filled with the sound of sledgehammers smashing against wood. My mother begged them to stop, but it was no use – with a colossal crack, the bolted door broke from the frame and the five men flew up the wooden steps. I heard my mother run after them, shouting at them to leave Miss Magpie alone . . .

And then came the strangest sound of all.

Silence.

I expected shouting. I expected to hear another fight. I listened for what felt like hours, trying to work out what was going on above me – but there was just . . . nothing.

I was about to give up when I finally heard a pair of footsteps race down the wooden steps. The door flew open and my mother ran inside. I knew instantly that something was wrong. She was as pale as a ghost.

'Get your things. We're leaving.'

'But—'

'*Now.*'

I knew that voice – I knew not to argue. I had never seen her look so frightened before. We packed our bags and left without looking back.

We spent Christmas with my aunt, sleeping on the floor of her apartment. When the New Year came we moved to another city – and that was that. We left everything behind. My mother refused to go back to the old building.

She was never the same after that Christmas. I asked her again and again what had happened in Miss Magpie's attic – I must have asked a hundred times. But my mother never said anything. I had no idea what happened that day to make my mother change so utterly, so quickly. It made me hate Christmas – despise it.

It was only much later in life – when my mother died, in fact – that I found out the full story. At the funeral I asked my aunt if Mother had ever spoken about what happened in Miss Magpie's attic – and to my amazement, my aunt said that she did.

'But a lot of it just . . . didn't make any

sense,' she explained apologetically. 'To be honest, I thought your mother had gone mad.'

'What do you mean?' I said.

She told me everything she knew. The landlord and his cronies had run into the attic and my mother had followed them. She was trying to stop them before they did something terrible to Miss Magpie – but when she reached the top of the stairs, she couldn't believe what she saw.

The attic was completely empty. It was a single dark room that ran from one end of the building to the other. At the far end, a great hole was torn in the roof. Wind was blowing through and leaving great flurries of snow on the attic floor; in the distance, the city cathedral was tolling the hour.

There was no furniture, not even a bed. Just a carpet of dried leaves and tiny bones on the floor. In fact, my mother noticed there were lots of bones. Piles of them.

'Well, don't just stand there!' the landlord shouted to his friends. 'The old bat has to be round here somewhere!'

But she wasn't – Miss Magpie was nowhere to be seen. It wasn't the house of an old lady – it was like the cave of some great monster. There were great gouges and scratches in rafters – some as wide as her hand. And the smell, my mother said – the *stench* . . .

'Over here!'

One of the men had found something in the darkest corner of the attic. It was a filthy rag curtain, strung with wire from the rafters. There was something hidden behind it – a stack of dead twigs. There were *sounds* coming from it, too. One of the men shone his torch inside.

It was a nest.

My mother never spoke about what she saw inside it – she simply refused to talk about it, right up until she died. And although I found the police report of what happened afterwards, it seemed none of the other men had wanted to describe what they had seen, either.

But they all agreed on what happened next. The landlord had taken one look at what was in the nest and turned ghost-white.

'What … what *are* those things?' he said, his voice trembling. 'Get rid of them!'

The men had refused – no one wanted to go anywhere near them. But the landlord was revolted by what he saw in the nest. It touched some part of himself and petrified him – something that threatened to get beneath his polished fingernails.

'I want them out of here!' he cried. 'Now!'

His friends refused. So the landlord did it himself. He grabbed a sledgehammer, emptied the nest – and killed the things inside it right there and then on the attic floor.

After that, everyone left – no one wanted to be near that room any more. The landlord was shaken and said he felt too sick to make his way home. Instead, he decided to spend the night in one of the newly vacated rooms on the floor below – there were plenty of them to choose from, since he had thrown out all his tenants. He told his friends he'd call them the next day.

It was the last time anyone saw him. When his friends hadn't heard from the landlord in a week they came to the building and broke down the door of the flat he'd stayed in.

All the furniture was smashed. The bed had been ripped to pieces. The wallpaper hung from the walls in shreds. Instead of a window there was a huge, gaping hole torn in the wall. A blizzard was filling the room with snow. You could hear carollers singing outside.

There was no sign of the landlord. According to the police report, there was no sign of anything left in the attic either: no tiny bones, no nest, and certainly no Miss Magpie. It seemed like she had disappeared, too – but there was no attempt to investigate where she had gone. No one, it seemed, wanted to pry too hard.

But there was one detail in the report that stayed with me long after I stopped reading. When one of the policemen had searched the landlord's bedroom the next day, he had noticed something *unusual* sticking out of the wooden frame of the shattered windows.

It was impossible for him to be certain – they were stuck too deep in the wood for that – but in the light, they almost looked like ten polished fingernails. Like someone had been gripping onto the window frame.

Like they been clutching on for dear life while something huge and monstrous dragged them out by force. Like they had held on until their fingernails finally ripped free, one by one, and the monster had carried them into the dark winter night.

The guests shrieked and applauded.

'Gin! Gin! Gin!'

Lewis charged round the table, emptying another two bottles into the guests' swaying glasses. By now, they were beginning to look worse for wear – rocking in their seats, the floor beneath them littered with empty bottles. Only the Dean stayed cold and sober, his eyes fixed on Lewis like a hawk.

He's up to something, *thought Lewis.* There *must* be some reason he's not drinking – but how will I ever be able to escape if he stays sober?

The clock struck four, and the Cook emerged with an enormous metal trolley. A tall figure stood on top of it, hidden from view by a long black rag. The Dean smashed another bauble and held up the name within.

'Now is the turn of Bloodrick Gallant – our expert in Disgusting Beasts and How to Cook Them!'

A man stood up and lit a cigar – the one who had almost crushed Lewis with a motorcycle earlier. Without his helmet you could see he had a shrivelled red head with dusty hair and watery eyes, like something left to bake in the sun.

'Come on, rat!' he snarled at Lewis. 'Show 'em my course!'

Lewis whipped off the covering, and the table gasped. Underneath it was a whole roast pig, with an apple stuffed in its mouth. But this was no ordinary roast pig. It hung by its neck on a creaking gallows, swinging on a noose made of sausages and dressed as Father Christmas. His sack was stuffed with giblets, and his rancid beard dribbled with hot fat. The smell was indescribable.

'Quite something, isn't it?' said Gallant. 'Nothing like the taste of an animal you've hunted and killed yourself! Of course, there's one *beast I've never managed to capture – one that's haunted me all my life.'*

He cast a desultory glance at Ariadne Biter.

'That's right – my *story happened to me as well. But unlike* some *people, I faced my monster head on!'*

He turned to the guests and told his gruesome story as the carcass cast its shadow across the table.

The Beast

We used to visit my grandfather's house every Christmas – then he died, and we never went again. I don't remember much about my childhood, but I remember his dark stone mansion. I remember the windowless rooms and cold gloomy ceilings. I remember the Christmas candles that burned in every room and somehow made the shadows even darker. But more than anything, I remember his animal collection.

They weren't *living* animals, of course – they were dead and stuffed, every one. My grandfather collected them by the thousand. Their heads covered every wall and their bodies were nailed to plinths in every corner. There were dead birds, dead moose, dead bears, dead lions – a whole dead whale hung suspended above the dining-room table. No matter where you walked in the house, a hundred glass eyeballs followed you.

But there was *one* room that my brother and I were forbidden to enter – my grandfather's study. We weren't even allowed to set foot on the corridor which led to it. I tried to sneak up there once, but I was caught out by the treacherous creaky step at the top of the staircase. It didn't so much *creak* as scream blue murder when you stepped on it – within seconds, my grandfather had found me and chased me twice round the garden with a bullwhip. He was a violent man with a foul temper – we all went out of our way to make sure we didn't encourage it.

Except, of course, for my brother.

'You mean you've *never* snuck inside his study?' he teased me one day. 'Ha! You're an even bigger baby than I thought you were!'

I scowled. 'I'm not a baby.'

'You should see what he keeps in there!' said my brother. 'We could sneak in right now and see . . . or are you too much of a coward?'

I wasn't a coward – but I *was* terrified of my grandfather. Just the thought of being caught in his forbidden room sent shivers up my spine. But curiosity and pride got the better of me, and after only a minute of teasing I caved.

We waited until the rest of my family had gone outside for lunch, then snuck into the main hall. Hanging from the neck of a marabou stork at the bottom of the staircase was the brass ring of keys that opened every door in the house. I lifted them off with a shaking hand – they felt heavier than I expected.

'Quick!' said my brother. 'We don't have much time – and don't forget about that creaky step!'

I followed him up the staircase, leaping expertly over the top step and down the long, dark corridor. The study door lay at the end of it. I made my way to the door on shaking legs, desperate to hide how frightened I was.

I unlocked the study and stepped inside. It was as I expected. There was a desk made of thick dark wood in the centre: more of a monument than a table. The walls on every side were lined with glass cabinets, and inside were hundreds more stuffed animals.

But these were no *ordinary* stuffed animals. These were curiosities – oddities – *mistakes*.

There were spineless fish, baby snakes coiled in jars, a hundred rat skeletons joined at the tail. Some were barely animals at all.

'Those are nothing,' said my brother. 'Come look at *this*.'

He stood beside another cabinet in the darkest corner of the room. It was covered with a blood-red curtain, which stood tall and steady like a waiting guest. My guts crawled just looking at it.

'What's under the curtain?' I asked nervously.

'See for yourself,' said my brother.

I couldn't say no. I walked up to the cabinet, swallowed hard, and pulled away the curtain.

The sight inside the cabinet almost made me retch. It was a man – at least, it *used* to be a man. He was long dead. His skin had sucked against his bones and turned his eyes into hollow caves. His lips had shrivelled to a grimace on his teeth. His arms and legs were held up by strings so he dangled inside the cabinet like a marionette.

'Gruesome, eh?' said my brother. 'Keeping dead animals in your house is one thing, but dead *murderers* . . .'

I gulped. 'M–Murderer?'

My brother tapped the brass plaque on the front of the cabinet. THE BEAST.

'He was a child killer,' my brother explained. 'Mothers used to tell their children, "You be good, or else the Beast will crawl through your window and get you!" '

I shuddered. 'That's not true.'

'It is so!' said my brother. '*Everyone* knew about the Beast – he was famous! When the police finally killed him, people refused to believe he was really dead. They said his body was still wandering the streets at night, searching for children . . .'

I glanced down. I'd stepped away from the cabinet without even realising it.

'So the police came up with an idea,' said my brother. 'To prove to everyone that the Beast *was* dead, they dug up his body and stuffed him full of paraffin wax.'

I grimaced. '*Paraffin wax?*'

'So the body wouldn't rot,' my brother explained. 'Then they took it on tour round the country – and look! They even cut off his feet to prove he couldn't walk anywhere! See?'

My brother pointed down to where the man's feet should be. True enough, the scrawny legs ended just above the ankle. They were thin and brittle as sticks.

'People came from all over the world to see his body,' said my brother. 'And some paid extra so they could touch him . . . Hey! That gives me an idea!'

He grabbed the keys off me and unlocked

the padlock on the cabinet.

I gasped. 'What are you doing?'

'Come on – don't you want to know what a dead murderer feels like?' said my brother.

I didn't – not one bit. But my brother couldn't be stopped. He swung open the glass door and stepped back. The first thing that hit me was the haze of the paraffin, emptying into the room like a fug.

'Phew – it's worse than petrol!' said my brother, waving the air. 'No wonder the old man keeps him locked up – one spark and he'd go up like a furnace!'

'Close the door,' I begged. 'Please – Grandfather could be up here any moment. If he smells *that*, we're done for!'

'Not till you touch him,' said my brother with an evil grin.

I was horrified. '*No!*'

My brother gave a sorry shake of his head.

'I knew it – you're a coward. Always were, and always will be.'

Something inside me boiled up. I knew what would happen if I refused – he'd hold it over me for the rest of my life. I couldn't let that happen. I turned to the shrivelled corpse in front of me, reached out an unsteady hand . . . and touched his arm.

A wave of disgust flooded through me. The skin had a glossy sheen like wax – but underneath it, the Beast was as dry as old canvas. He almost crackled beneath your fingers.

'HELLFIRE! WHERE IN DAMNATION ARE THOSE BOYS?'

My brother and I swung round in horror. Our grandfather had come back in the house. My brother threw the keys at me, all bravery gone in a flash.

'Quick! Cover him up!'

He slammed the cabinet door closed and I threw the blood-red curtain back over the top. In seconds we were out of the room, locking the door behind us and charging down the stairs – only just remembering at the last second to leap over the creaking stair. I flung the keys back over the stork's neck just as grandfather appeared in the hallway.

'THERE YOU ARE!' he bellowed. 'OUTSIDE, BEFORE I FLOG YOU BOTH WITH MY BELT!'

I breathed a sigh of relief. We had gotten away with it – just – and best of all, I had proved I wasn't a coward. Now my brother would finally leave me alone. I would never need to go back into grandfather's study and see that gruesome, shrivelled face ever again.

How wrong I was.

*

'Wake up!'

It was midnight. The first thing I saw when I opened my eyes was my brother's face, staring down at me in the light of a shaking candle. I rubbed my eyes.

'What's wrong?'

My brother heaved me out of bed. '*The cabinet, you idiot!* I just realised – you didn't lock it behind you!'

My stomach plummeted. My brother was right. If my grandfather found the padlock had been taken off his cabinet, then we were both done for.

'What do we do?' I whispered.

'*We?*' said my brother. 'You had the keys – it was your job to lock it! Go back and do it, now!'

I tried to point out that my brother was the one who opened it in the first place – but it was no use. He was bigger, meaner, and crueller than me – and he was even more scared than I was. Every protest was met by a barrage of threats and punches. I had no choice – I was going to have to go back to the study and lock the cabinet myself.

I took the candle and crept through the house. It was completely silent now – not even our grandfather was awake. Walking through the house was like walking through another world of darkness. On every side a host of dead animals gazed down at me, their eyes glimmering and their faces half cast in shadow.

I crept into the hall and carefully lifted the keys from the stork's neck. They seemed even heavier in my hand now. I crept up the staircase, avoiding the stares of a thousand dead animals around me. I tried not to think of the face of the Beast in the cabinet, waiting for me to lift the curtain—

CREEEEEAK.

I'd forgotten about the top step.

The sound echoed through the hall and bounced off the walls. I stood frozen to the spot with terror – surely my grandfather must have heard it? *Surely* he was going to come running out of his bedroom any second like a madman, waving his bullwhip and shrieking?

But there was nothing – just the steady, still death of the house around me. I released my foot inch by inch, feeling every creak and groan of the wood like a bone snapping in my leg until I could finally lift it from the step and make my way down the corridor.

My hands were slick with sweat as I unlocked the study door. Inside the room was as dark as you could expect – I felt like I was exploring the sunken hull of a shipwreck. The flickering candle in my hand glanced off the glass in the cabinets and made the monsters inside look like they were moving.

I turned to the blood-red curtain in the corner. It stood waiting for me, still and silent.

I steeled myself as much as I could, but the candle shook in my hand, making shadows dance around the cabinet. I tried not to imagine what the Beast's face would look like when I pulled back the curtain. I tried not to imagine how the candlelight would shimmer off his greasy skin. I tried not to imagine the moment when I would reach out for the padlock, only for his bony arm to snap forward and grab my wrist—

I shook my head. There was no use frightening myself like this – I had to do the job and get out, fast. I took a deep breath, marched across the room and whipped off the curtain.

The cabinet was empty.

My mind reeled. The Beast was gone. How was that possible? Had he been stolen? Had he—

CREEEEAK.

The sound had come from the end of the corridor.

Something had just stepped on the top of the stairs.

My blood froze. I couldn't move – I could barely even breathe. The study door lay open in front of me, but there was only darkness beyond it. I knew deep down that there couldn't – *shouldn't* – be anything there. There was no way that the Beast was walking the house while everyone slept. There was no way a dead man could be coming up the stairs to get me. I told myself that it was simply my grandfather out there in the darkness, come to give me the thrashing of a lifetime.

But no. I could hear another sound now, coming down the corridor towards me, growing louder and louder ... and it didn't sound like my grandfather's footsteps. It sounded like two dry sticks being dragged across the carpet.

A figure slowly emerged from the darkness ahead. I could barely see it in the candlelight – it was little more than an outline. But I could see that it was tall and thin. I could see that its head was bowed. I could see that it was clawing along the walls to steady itself. I could see that it had no feet.

The figure stopped. I watched as it lifted its head to face me, staring at me with its empty, gaping sockets, the dead, dry skin crackling as it moved . . .

And there in front of me was the Beast from the cabinet.

I was paralysed with horror. The Beast stared at me for what felt like an eternity. Then it opened its lipless mouth with another crackle of dry skin, revealing the gleaming teeth behind it . . .

'*Booooooy*,' he croaked with delight.

He fell forwards – only he wasn't falling. He was coming for me, quicker than I could ever have imagined, his arms outstretched and his stumps scuttling across the carpet like a spider.

I did the only thing I could think of – I screamed with terror and swung the ring of keys at him. They struck him hard on the side of the head, and with a terrible rip his head tore clean from his neck. No, not clean – it hung upside down at his chest, still connected by a fragment of oily skin, rolling and bouncing off his ribcage as the empty sockets glared at me with rage.

'BOOOOOOOOOOY!'

His hand whipped out and grabbed me – he had me by the hair. He pulled me closer to the terrible mouth, covering me with a wave of paraffin . . .

One spark and he'd go up like a furnace.

And suddenly I knew what to do. I raised the burning candle and plunged it deep into his ribcage.

The skin caved in like paper. The Beast stared at me in shock – then a sound came from inside him like nothing I'd ever heard before. A shriek so high and piercing that I almost felt my brains rattle against my skull. He threw himself back, the fire catching on his parchment skin like a bonfire and spreading through the paraffin wax in his body. In seconds, he was a raging torch. The room lit up … and I realised with horror that we weren't alone. The things inside the cabinets – the jars of snakes, the conjoined rats, the headless birds – were alive too, writhing and clawing to escape from the glass. I raced out of the study, flying down the dark corridor as fast as I could.

There was another scream behind me –

a scream of furious agony. The Beast was still coming for me – but he wasn't on his feet any more. He was dragging himself down the corridor on all fours, burning like an inferno with his arms outstretched. Paraffin gushed from his eyes and nose and mouth in floods and poured onto the carpet beneath him.

'BOOOOOOOOOOOY!'

His body was falling apart, but the fire wasn't stopping him. The corridor around him was on fire. The flames spread fast across the paraffin-soaked carpet, licking up to the rows of stuffed heads on the wall – and I realised with horror that they were alive, too. They were craning their necks and bellowing, trying to get away from the flames. The ones on plinths were trying to pull their legs from the stands they were nailed to. They weren't really dead. They were alive – all of them.

'Fire! Fire!' I cried, charging down the

stairs. '*Everyone out, quick—*'

I stopped dead. My grandfather was standing in the hall ahead of me.

He wasn't looking at the flames eating up the house around him. He wasn't looking at the thousands of screaming animals that had somehow come alive on his walls, shrieking and writhing with fear. He wasn't even looking at the flaming corpse of the Beast as it crawled down the staircase towards me.

He was looking at me. And maybe I was mad with terror – maybe I was even poisoned by wood smoke – but I swear on my life that he had no eyes. They were two gaping sockets in his head – just like the Beast.

'My house,' he whispered. 'What have you done to my house?'

I fled into the winter night, away from the house and the horrors inside it, and I didn't stop running until dawn.

*

When the police finally found me the next day, I was collapsed in the snow by the side of the road, a gibbering wreck. I had run all night and I was mad with exhaustion. They had to give me a sedative to stop me screaming before they could take me to the hospital.

When I finally came to, the police explained what had happened. My grandfather's house had burned to the ground. My mother, father and brother had all escaped the fire in time – but not my grandfather. He had perished in the flames, along with all his possessions. The antiques, the paintings, the animals . . . they were completely destroyed. Nothing was left.

'Was there anyone else in the house at the time?' the police asked me. 'Any other relatives, some servants, maybe?'

I shook my head.

Strange, said the police – we found another set of footsteps in the snow, you see, right beside yours. They led us right to you – in fact, it was almost like someone had been following you. But these other footsteps … well, they didn't look like *feet*.

They looked like someone had been walking on a set of sticks.

Bloodrick finished his story to rapturous applause. The guests had stripped the pig down to its bare bones, and its skeleton swung murderously in the firelight. Lewis emptied two more bottles into their swaying glasses.

You're running out of time, *he whispered to himself.* Quick – you have to think of some way to get them fighting again! But how can you possibly escape without the Dean seeing . . . ?

The clock struck five. The Dean smashed the

penultimate bauble and held up the piece of paper. There was a flicker of surprise on his face.

'Well – here's something unexpected. It seems our next storyteller is . . . Drybone Creathe. Our Advisor in Infernal Law!'

The guests murmured uncertainly and turned to the end of the table.

The man standing up was calm and quiet – after everything Lewis had seen that night, that seemed strange in itself. But the more you looked at him, the more you noticed how blank *he was – he was like a darkened room that slowly reveals itself to be empty. There wasn't a single trace of emotion on his face – not in his eyes, nor in his speech or movements. He hid one hand inside his shirt, clutching at his chest like something there pained him.*

The Cook booted open the doors. Balanced in his hands was the biggest Christmas pudding Lewis had ever seen: a vast black orb, towering over the guests like a dark moon. The Cook struggled under its weight, his already hunched back doubled over as he carried it to the table.

'Well, boy?'

Creathe's voice was cold and grey as a tomb. He held out a burning torch.

'Light it.'

The guests cackled and rubbed their hands with glee. Lewis took the torch with shaking hands. He had no idea what was going to happen – whether the pudding was going to explode in his face, or if the torch would suddenly burn him to a crisp . . . perhaps he *was going to be the final course, served up burnt and bubbling on a plate?*

The guests were silent with anticipation as Lewis approached the pudding. He held out the torch—

Then stopped. The wooden table in front of him was slick with gin.

I could set it on fire – just like in the last story! *thought Lewis.* This whole table would go up like a rocket! I could escape in the confusion and—

From the other end of the table, the Dean caught his eye. He had the faintest smile on his lips – and he was shaking his head.

No, boy.

Lewis froze. The Dean knew exactly what Lewis was thinking – that he was trying to escape. And the worst part was, he wasn't worried in the slightest. He was giving him a look that said: We're not done yet.

'Light the pudding, boy,' said the Dean.

Lewis held the torch to the pudding, and it erupted into flames. The heat that came off it was extraordinary: the air in the dining hall shimmered. Drybone Creathe's cold, blank face was illuminated in the glare – but it still showed absolutely nothing.

'I was a young man when I went to Cu Sith. I was working as a debt collector at the time. I never imagined that when I left that terrible island, I would be the one who came away with less than what I arrived with.'

He winced – the hand clutched even tighter at his chest. The moment passed – the fire on the pudding slowly died. Creathe turned his back to the guests, and faced the fireplace.

'There's a prize inside the pudding. Whoever finds it can keep it – all I ask is that you listen to my story.'

The guests tore frenziedly into the smoking pudding on the table, while Drybone told his tale to the fire.

Black Dog

I had just started in the debt-collecting business when my boss called me to his office. It was December 23rd: there was no one else left in the building. Outside a handful of carollers sang ancient songs in the fog.

'I've heard good things about you, boy,' said my boss, eyeing me over his polished desk. 'They say nothing scares you. You can get money off *anyone* without breaking a sweat!'

It was true – I had worked hard to earn my reputation. When people are frightened of you, they hand over their money much faster.

'That's exactly what I need for this next job,' said my boss, leaning back in his chair. 'It's a tough one – *very* tough, in fact. Normally I wouldn't ask someone so new to take it on, but all my best men are gone for the holidays.' He thumped a fist on the desk. 'Damn Christmas! You don't have any plans, do you?'

I was going to spend Christmas Day in my bedsit, poisoning the rats. 'Nothing I can't change, sir.'

My boss nodded approvingly. 'Good to hear it! We'll put you on the next train up north before the railway shuts down for Christmas. You'll be on the coast by tomorrow morning!'

I was confused. 'Coast, sir?'

My boss turned to the window. I could see his face in the reflection, peering out the fog.

'One of our oldest clients died last year. He owed us *thousands* – we've been trying to claim back what we can. We're selling off all his assets, but we're having trouble getting rid of one of the islands he owns – goes by the name of Cu Sith. Ever heard of it?'

I shook my head.

'Of course you haven't!' My boss laughed. 'No one has – thirty miles off the cold north coast and nothing but water on every side as far as the eye can see. No streets, no trees . . . they don't even have electricity, so far as I can tell. There's only one family left, but it seems no one wants to buy the island while they're still on it.' He shuddered. 'I've seen pictures of that godforsaken place. Why anyone would choose to live there is a mystery to me.'

He started organising some papers.

'I need you to travel to Cu Sith and evict the family straightaway – threaten them with some made-up legal action, that sort of thing. Afterwards you'll have to stay on the island for a few days to make sure they don't attempt to sneak back in the house. I'll send a couple more men up on Boxing Day when the trains start running.' He glanced at me. 'Sure you don't mind spending Christmas alone?'

I shook my head. 'I won't let you down, sir.'

My boss gave me a look.

'Glad to see such enthusiasm. But be careful, boy – I doubt that family will take kindly to being kicked off their island on Christmas Eve. That far out in the middle of nowhere . . . well, no one will be around to help you if things turn nasty, let me put it that way.'

Within the hour I was on the last train up north. It was deepest midwinter and a chilling fog clawed through the windows, turning the carriage into an icebox. The darkness outside grew thicker and heavier with every mile.

I let the carriage rattle me back and forth and prepared for what was ahead of me. I tried to imagine Cu Sith – was it really as bad as my boss described? Should I have been more afraid?

I clutched the revolver in my pocket. Normally I would never have taken it out of my bedsit – but something about the look on my boss's face when he talked about the family had made me think twice about what I was getting into.

I arrived at the north coast early on Christmas Eve, and headed straight to the harbour. It was a small fishing village, and desperately poor.

Perfect, I thought. *That means more people willing to take me out at a moment's notice. I might even be able to short-change them!*

But I was wrong. No one – absolutely no one – was willing to go to Cu Sith, no matter how much money I offered. At the first mention of the island the fishermen would stop the conversation.

'No – we've got no business going there. And neither should you, if you know what's good for you.'

Then they would simply turn away. Nothing I could say would make them start talking to me again – it was like I was already dead.

Finally, just when I was about to give up, a young fisherman came over to me.

'They say you want to get to Cu Sith,' he said.

My eyes lit up. 'Yes! Can you take me?'

The fisherman looked at me warily.

'What are you wanting with . . . that place?'

I shifted on my feet. Something about the way he said 'that place' unnerved me.

'I have business with the family,' I

explained. 'I need to get there straightaway. I'll pay you handsomely for it.'

I showed him my full money clip. It was far more than I'd intended to pay, but at this point I was desperate. This young fisherman might well be the only person left who was willing to make the journey. I couldn't let him get away.

The fisherman looked at the money, his face torn. 'I–I'll take you. But we'll have to leave right away. There's a storm coming – I want to be back before it hits.'

'You could always stay on Cu Sith till it passes,' I suggested.

I'll never forget the look on the man's face when I said it. Without another word, he turned round and walked away.

We left immediately. Despite the approaching storm it was a calm morning, and the sea was as flat as glass as we sped out of the harbour. A winter sunrise had filled the sky behind us, sparkling on the waves like angels. I watched the mainland slip away for what felt like hours, amazed by how beautiful it was.

In fact I was so transfixed that when the fisherman finally spoke it made me jump.

'Up ahead.'

I turned round – and was shocked by what I saw. The beautiful weather stopped instantly. The sky ahead was as grey as an unmarked gravestone: a blizzard covered the ocean as far as the eye could see. The waves reared up like dogs.

Cu Sith.

I could just make it out through the snow. It was as flat and grey as the sky: a patch of barren rock lashed by sea winds. It looked like the sun had never once shone on it.

'People *live* here?' I said in disbelief.

The fisherman nodded gravely and pointed to the only house on the island. It was little more than a box, the same colour as the stones it stood on, dotted with grim little windows. But bigger than I expected – much bigger. Three whole floors above the ground, with an enormous chimney on the roof.

'Good grief,' I said. 'It looks more like a church.'

The fisherman scuffed his feet beside me. I got the feeling – not for the first time – that there was something he was desperate to ask me. It might well have been the only reason he agreed to take me on the journey in the first place.

'Sir – forgive me for asking, but what business do you have here? What could you possibly want with those . . . people?'

I sighed. It was time to tell him the truth.

'You know the family that lives here?'

The fisherman's eyes darkened. 'We all know them, sir.'

I picked up my briefcase. 'Well, I work for a company which owns Cu Sith. I've been asked to evict the family – that means 'kick them out' – and make sure they stay out. I'll be staying in the house by myself until my colleagues arrive on Boxing Day morning. In fact – I have another job for you, if you're interested.'

I pulled another wad of banknotes from my briefcase, even bigger than the last one.

'I need to get the family off the island as quickly as possible. If you take them back to the mainland for me, I'll pay you treble what you've earned already. So long as you don't mind waiting here for a little bit, I . . .'

I trailed off. The fisherman had turned ghost-white – he was practically shaking. Without another word he threw the anchor overboard and heaved a plank of sodden wood between the rocks and the boat.

'No – not interested!' he cried. 'You need to go – storm's coming!'

I was shocked by the sudden change in his manner. 'I can offer you more if—'

'NO!'

For a moment, I genuinely thought he was going to strike me. I picked up my things and scurried across the plank as quick as I could. The fisherman sped away without so much as a glance behind him.

I watched him go, stunned. He had been terrified – genuinely terrified. The suggestion of being anywhere *near* that family was enough to send him running.

And now I was alone with them.

I faced the giant house – and felt a clutch at my chest.

They were there, standing outside. Waiting for me.

I had never seen anything quite like them.

There were six in total – a husband, a wife and four children. Clothed in rags, sick and dirty. Above all, they looked hungry – *starving*.

That wasn't the strangest thing about them. Their skin, their clothes, their eyes: they were all the same colour as the island. The dull, grey of ash and decay. The only exception was their lips: they were a bright, vivid red, like a deep slash in the middle of their faces.

I wanted to run. I wanted to swim my way back to the mainland – but I knew I couldn't. The blizzard was coming thick and fast. I had to stand my ground and get the family off the island, quick. I gripped the revolver in my pocket, wrapped my coat and scarf tight around me, and made my way to the house.

Every footstep on the snow was like a gunshot – *crunch, crunch, crunch, crunch* – echoing out around me with impossible loudness. It seemed like it was the only sound in the world. The family stared at me in blank silence the whole time – no hatred, no curiosity, watching as I drew closer and closer.

Finally I stood in front of them. The father was a giant: twice my size at least. His blood-red mouth hung open. He had no teeth.

'What do you want?' he growled.

I cleared my throat. I couldn't look afraid – not now.

'I'm from a debt collection agency,' I said. 'We own the rights to Cu Sith and all the property on it – including your house. I have all the paperwork right here.'

I considered taking a sheet out of my briefcase to show them – but changed my mind. I had no idea if the family could even read.

'You need to leave the island immediately,' I said. 'You will show me inside the house, hand over the keys, and never return. From now on, all your property inside it belongs to the agency. Any refusal to leave will result in your immediate arrest, and . . . and . . .'

The idiocy of what I was saying to them suddenly struck me. This family may never even have seen a police officer before – what would they care about a court of law? It was me against six of them – even with the revolver, I wouldn't stand a chance if they attacked me. No wonder the fisherman had refused to stay – I was clearly in over my head. The handle of the gun felt wet and sticky in my hand.

Then – just like that – the father pushed his youngest boy forward.

'You heard the man, John. Show him inside.'

I was shocked. I had expected refusal – shouting – violence. Not this.

'Really? You're sure you don't mind leaving so—'

'Be quick, John,' said the father, cutting me off. 'We have to leave before it gets dark.'

John wordlessly took my hand and led me to the door. It was as simple as that – like they *wanted* me to take the island off them. I took one last, confused glance at the family – they stood exactly where I'd left them on the snow, watching me in silence like ghosts.

I let John lead me through the house, room by room. Inside was even worse than I'd expected. The house had been built to withstand sea winds and brutal winters: there was no room for comfort here. The corners of every room were stagnant with filth, and every surface was covered in a film of grimy sea salt.

I gazed at the cramped, dingy rooms in disgust. The thought of spending two days by myself here was becoming less and less appealing by the second. Just as my boss had said, there was no electricity or running water. They didn't even have a fireplace in the—

I stopped.

'Where's the fireplace?'

The boy blinked. 'We don't have a fireplace.'

I fixed him with a look.

'John – you're lying to me. There's an enormous chimney on the roof. That means there *must* be a fireplace somewhere. Where is it?'

John looked petrified. I grinned – I'd struck gold.

'Are your family hiding something from me, John?'

It all made sense now. No wonder the family had been so unconcerned about leaving – they had everything stashed in a secret room somewhere! If there *was* anything valuable hidden here, I couldn't let them sneak back in and take it while I slept. Hand a secret stash of riches over to the boss, and a promotion was as good as mine. I knelt down in front of John and pulled a sparkling penny out my pocket.

'John, show me where the fireplace is and this coin is yours.'

The boy's eyes lit up. He glanced over his shoulder – as if he could see his family watching him through the wall.

'There's . . . a basement,' he said quietly. 'But we're not supposed to go down there.'

He reached out to take the coin, but I snatched it away.

'Show me.'

John couldn't refuse. He led me to a back room and opened a door. At first, it seemed like an ordinary closet – but as John moved aside some boxes, I realised that there was another door hidden at the back, locked tight with five massive bolts. John swung the door open, revealing a set of cold stone steps that led down into darkness.

I didn't waste a moment. I pushed John aside and tore down the stairs, expecting to see heaps of shipwrecked riches ... but there was nothing. The room was an empty square. Nothing but four stone walls and a pounded-dirt floor.

'There's the fireplace,' said John.

As if I could miss it – it took up the entire end wall. It was made of grey stone and decorated with straw figures, hammered into the stone with iron nails.

'Christmas decorations?' I smirked. 'Not exactly the most festive room, is it John?'

I stepped closer to the decorations and pulled one off the wall. It was filthy – like it'd been made years ago. In fact, the more I looked at it the more it seemed—

I gagged. This was no Christmas decoration – there were human teeth in it. Bits of fingernail, too. I threw it into the fireplace in horror.

'What the hell are these? Why have you hung them above a fireplace in an empty—'

I stopped. I had just seen the inside of the fireplace. The stone was scorched black. It was covered in nail marks.

'They're not for us,' said John. 'They're for Black Dog.'

I blinked. '*Black Dog?*'

'Black Dog that comes down the chimney.'

That was it. He just kept staring at me, as if what he said made complete sense. I kept my breath held for what felt like a very long time. I realised that I was afraid to ask the question.

'John ... are your family *really* the only people on this island?'

'JOHN!'

The shout came from outside – the father. John turned white and bolted back up the stairs before I could stop him. His family were exactly where we had left them – they hadn't moved an inch. I caught the boy just before he flew out the front door.

'John,' I whispered. 'What's going on? What are you hiding from me?'

'I . . . I can't tell you!'

He was terrified – just like the fisherman. I gripped his arm tight.

'John, you *have* to tell me what's going on. Am I safe here tonight?'

The boy swallowed, his eyes darting back outside. 'You . . . you're really going to stay in the house? By yourself?'

I nodded. John turned to the door, his face

torn. Finally he leaned forward and hissed in my ear.

'You have to lock the door. Lock it tight so nothing gets in. If you don't, then—'

'JOHN!'

John flew out without another word. I watched in shock as he rejoined the family and the six of them walked away from the house. They kept their gaze fixed on the wide, grey sea ahead. Only John turned to look back at me – just once. I could see pure terror in the whites of his eyes.

I closed the door . . . and only then allowed myself to become frightened. I had no idea what I had let myself in for – but John's message was clear. I wasn't safe. The family – or someone else – were going to come back in the night and get me. I probably had a few hours of daylight left before the island turned dark. Before then, I had to turn the house into a fortress.

I locked the door, just like John had said, and piled every piece of furniture I could find against it. I broke apart the table and nailed the wood over the windows. I barricaded the bottom of the staircase with wooden chairs, boxes, benches – anything that might work as an obstacle – then holed myself up in the main bedroom at the top of the house.

I chose this room for one reason alone: it had two windows facing in different directions over the island. If anyone approached the house, it was my best chance to see them – I could even fire a warning shot out of the window and scare them away. The rest of the room was as barren and unpleasant as you would expect: a filthy bed piled high with rags in one corner, and a wall covered in great cracks from floor to ceiling. Behind it lay the great chimneypiece which ran from the basement to the roof: I could hear the wind whine through it as the blizzard grew closer.

I broke apart the bed and hammered the boards over the window frames, so that only the thinnest of grey lights could seep into the room. Before I had finished it, the snow had started to fall, hard. Wrapping myself in every blanket I could find I sank into a corner and watched the last dregs of sunlight die over Cu Sith.

I have no idea how long I sat there, watching and waiting. The room had a clock, but the hands had fallen off long ago – all it gave me was the slow, steady tock of unravelling time. Soon the dull grey of the blizzard faded into a crippling blackness – and when it did, the room became cold. *Deathly* cold.

I set to work lighting candles, sticking them to every surface of the bedroom until it lit up around me like a lantern. Outside the wind kept screaming madness and sent the window boards rattling. I sank back into the corner, the revolver clutched to my chest. I had never felt more scared in my life.

'Please God,' I whispered. 'Don't let me die here. Don't let me die on this miserable island. I'll give you whatever you want. Just don't let them get me. Don't . . .'

I don't remember falling asleep. I do remember opening my eyes and seeing that all the candles had burned out – that I was surrounded by darkness. The blizzard had finally passed, and the wind had died. The windows weren't rattling any more.

That was why I could hear it.

Crunch, crunch. Crunch, crunch.

Someone was walking towards the house. No – two people. Two sets of footsteps in the snow.

I sat bolt upright, my heart racing. The family had come back for me. They were outside the house.

I ran to the boarded windows and looked outside. It was so dark I couldn't even make out the ground. The only sign of life were the footsteps, getting closer and closer to the house.

I lifted the revolver, ready to send out a warning shot. I only had six bullets. That meant I had to wait until they were right beneath me, right outside the front door. It was the only way I could scare them enough to ensure they'd run away. But leave it too late and— Well, it didn't even bear thinking about.

I silently removed one of the planks of wood over the window and stood in the pitch dark, holding out the revolver in trembling hands. My breath plumed in the frozen air. All I could do was listen.

Crunch, crunch, crunch, crunch.

The footsteps reached the front door.

Crunch.

And stopped.

For a long time there was nothing. No talking, no sound of the door being tested. I stood stock-still, trying to silence my heartbeat, trying to keep my nerves quiet and my gun steady and—

BOOM.

The sound came from above me, slamming on the roof.

I cried out in shock. There was something on the roof – and it was big. My brain reeled. The house was three storeys tall – how on earth could any one have jumped up there? And yet I could hear them even now, pounding across the roof tiles to the far corner of the room – two sets of footsteps in a close dance, making their way to the chimney . . .

I gasped. Suddenly all I could see was

John's face in the basement, his face blank and expressionless.

Black Dog that comes down the chimney.

Horror rose like a flood inside me. I wasn't hearing two sets of footsteps. It was something on four legs.

I turned to the chimney on the wall – and cried out with a sickening, gut-white fear. The bricks were swelling and splitting right in front of me. Something was forcing its way down the chimney and inside the house. A new sound filled the room – claws scraping against stone. I could hear heavy gasping breaths through the wall, the bricks heaving like a chest as the monster dragged its way to the basement . . .

The basement that was bolted from the outside.

And suddenly there was John's face again, begging me with tears in his eyes.

You have to lock the door. Lock it tight so nothing can get in.

He hadn't meant the front door. He'd meant the basement door. The door I had left open.

I had turned the house into a fortress – and I had locked myself inside it with a monster.

The house filled with a howl so loud and terrible that every hair on my body stood on end. The floor shuddered beneath my feet – the shudder of something huge and fast running up stairs.

Black Dog was coming for me.

I cried out in terror and threw the bedroom door shut. It had no lock – but that would make no difference here. The monster had heard me – I could hear it charging out of the basement and tearing through the ground floor to find me. There was nowhere left for me to go but the window.

I tore off the boards as fast as I could – but it wasn't fast enough. I could already hear Black Dog flying up the staircase, tearing apart the obstacles I had left in its path like they were matchsticks. It was already on the first floor, pounding up the second flight of stairs . . .

The last of the boards gave way. I ran my hand around the frame, looking for the handle – but there wasn't any. I gave a great groan of terror. The monster was on the second floor now, the sound of its feet hammering against the steps below me as it grew closer, the howl in its throat getting louder and louder . . .

I stepped back from the window and raised the revolver.

BLAM!

The blast shattered the glass and the room filled with freezing sea air just as the monster reached the final flight of stairs. I could hear its claws gouging through the wooden steps as it tore towards the bedroom door, its great heaving sides scraping against the walls and splitting the plaster . . .

I threw myself at the window at the exact moment the door exploded inwards. I shouldn't have turned back. I should have flung myself straight out the window and taken my chances with the ground. But I couldn't help myself. I couldn't help turning to see what had come for me from the darkness of Cu Sith – what it was that filled the door frame from edge to edge right now, with its foul black hair and bleeding eyes . . .

It was the worst mistake I ever made. The monster leapt at me in a single bound, its jaws wrenched open wide as I whipped round the gun and pulled the trigger . . .

I remember the pain. I remember the

muffled gunshot that seemed to come from somewhere far away. I remember the sensation of cold as I fell through the window and into the night air. I remember the snow on the ground as I landed, and how for a moment I thought that I could hear the waves themselves crashing on to the island, heaving themselves out of the black north ocean to claim me – until I realised it was footsteps. Running towards me on every side, getting closer.

It's them, I thought. *It's the family, come back for the final part of their sacrifice – to feed me to him, piece by piece.*

And the funny thing was – for a moment, lying there in the snow, staring up at the starless night as the footsteps drew closer – dying wasn't what frightened me the most. What frightened me most was knowing that no matter what the family did to me, no one would ever find my body. That there had been hundreds before me, and there would be hundreds more after. That I would spend my last living moment on Cu Sith – and then become another ancient myth, lost to the dark waters of time.

And my last thought before the darkness fell completely was – *what will they do to me in that basement?*

Drybone Creathe fell silent. He remained staring into the fire – no one could see his face.

'And then?' said the Dean. 'What happened next?'

Creathe didn't turn round. He kept his back to the table, facing the fire.

'When I woke up, I was in hospital on the mainland. It was New Year's Day: in front of me were the two men that my boss had sent to meet me.

'They explained what had happened: apparently when the young fisherman had returned to the harbour on Christmas Eve, there was uproar – no one could believe that he had taken me to Cu Sith and left me there. A handful of brave fisherman had waited for the storm to pass before coming to get me, right there and then in the middle of the night. They had found me lying on the snow outside the house, covered in blood. If they hadn't arrived when they did . . . well, who knows what could have happened to me.'

The Dean glanced at the other guests. They looked as confused as he was.

'And the monster?' he asked. 'Black Dog?'

Creathe shook his head, his hand still clutching at his chest.

'The house was empty – the whole island was empty, in fact. The family had disappeared. There was no explanation for what had

happened – nothing except my story, which sounded like the fantasies of a madman. The company didn't believe me, of course – why would they? Why believe a giant monster had come down the chimney to get me? The two men handed me my termination papers, and I never went back to work again.'

The guests had begun to lose interest in Creathe's story. One or two of them turned back to the enormous pudding on the table, searching through it for the missing prize.

'But there were one or two things which no one could explain,' said Creathe. 'For example, the state of the house. There was no way I could have torn through the wood of the floorboards like that – as if my hands were made of knives. And of course, how could anyone explain what they found in the centre of the pounded-dirt floor in the basement, surrounded by a ring of dead sea grass and covered in—'

The hall was filled by a high-pitched scream. Everyone spun round. Lady Arabella Dogspit, who had been wolfing the remains of her Christmas pudding, flew back from her seat in terror, flinging something away from her like a red-hot coal.

It was a human hand. It had been torn off at the wrist and stripped to gleaming bone – and clutched in its grip was a black revolver.

Another sound filled the hall now. It was Drybone Creathe, shrieking at the top of his voice. He had turned back to the table, but his face was no longer blank: it was contorted with insane laughter, his eyes wide and howling. He tore his arm from his shirt to show the ragged stump where his hand should be, where something years ago had torn it from him and never given it back.

At first the guests were stunned – but one by one, they joined in with Creathe's manic laughter. Soon they were pounding the tables and rolling over backwards – after a while even Lady Arabella was shrieking along. The Dean wiped tears from his eyes.

'Creathe, that's the first time I've seen you smile in forty years! And I do believe it might be the best surprise we've seen tonight!' He raised his glass. 'Come everyone, another toast! To the most gruesome, horrifying Christmas Dinner of Souls yet!'

Within seconds a flurry of forks and spoons and plates were flying through the air towards Lewis.

'Serving boy!'

'More gin, you miserable bag of filth!'

Lewis scrambled for the coffin-shaped cabinet in the corner.

One more story and I'm out of time, *he thought to himself.* What are they going to do to me then? I have to find a way out of here! Think, Lewis, think!

Lewis came to the cabinet – and stopped.

The cabinet was empty. There were no bottles of gin left.

'What are you waiting for, boy?' bellowed the Dean. 'Refill our glasses, now!'

Lewis turned to the table. A sea of cruel and evil faces met him in the firelight. His throat dried up. This was it – this was the moment they killed him.

'There's . . . there isn't any more,' he whispered. 'It's all gone.'

The effect on the room was cataclysmic. The guests leapt from their chairs like they had been electrocuted.

'No more gin?'

'The little maggot's guzzled it up for himself!'

'Get 'im!'

'Skin 'im!'

'Rip out his teeth!'

'NO!'

The Dean smashed his hand onto the table.

'Didn't you hear me the first time? No one touches the boy until after the Dinner is finished! We need him!' He turned to Lewis with an evil grin. 'Because we all *know what happens to the serving boy at the end of the night, don't we?'*

The guests broke into maniacal laughter once more. Lewis trembled from head to toe . . .

'That's right!' said Drybone Creathe. 'We make him clear up!'

Lewis blinked. Clear up?

'It'll take him forever,' *said Bloodrick Gallant gleefully. 'Look at this place! It's a tip!'*

'Just mopping the floor will take him most of Christmas morning,' said Ariadne Biter.

'And that says nothing for the laundry!' giggled Sir Algernon Thoroughbred-Pilt, grabbing the tablecloth. 'Oooh, these stains are going to be a nightmare!'

Lewis's face flooded with relief – that was it? They'd make him tidy up? After all this time, he'd been so worried – and all for nothing. He still had a chance to get out of here and stop these evil people, before they tried to destroy Christmas!

The clock struck six.

'Come!' said the Dean. 'Our night is not yet over. We still have one more story to hear.'

He broke the final bauble and held up the name.

'The last storyteller of the night is . . . myself.'

The guests stared at him in confusion.

'You?'

'But you're the Dean!'

'You've never . . .'

They trailed off. The Dean was staring at them, steady as a lighthouse. He gestured to their empty chairs.

'Well?'

One by one, the guests sat down, muttering with confusion. The Dean cleared his throat.

'Once upon a—'

'What about your course?' cried Retch Wallmanner. 'You're supposed to serve a course with your story!'

The Dean waved him quiet. 'Please, Retch, just listen to my story. All will become clear very soon.'

The Dean cleared his throat, and began his tale.

The Dean's Tale

'Once upon a time, there was a miserable old Dean of a miserable old College in a miserable old village. He hated his job, hated his life – but more than anything, he hated the filthy, foul-mouthed morons who he was forced to work with day in, day out!

'The Dean suffered these dreadful people for one reason alone: he wanted to get his hands on the Dead Man's Jabberers. Like the others, he longed to claim them for himself and become the Lord of Darkness; but he didn't just want to use their evil power to bring down *Christmas* – oh no! The Dean was much more ambitious than that. He wanted to bring the whole world to its knees. He wanted nothing more than to rule all mankind with terror until the end of time – an immortal god of fear!

'The desire consumed him night and day. He barely ate, he barely slept. All he did was read, read, read, hoping to find some way that he could claim the teeth for himself. But how? The Dean was no storyteller – he would never be chosen as a winner at the Christmas Dinner of Souls. And besides, what if he wasn't worthy of the Dead Man's Jabberers? The teeth would kill him the second he tried to wear them!

'But one day – earlier this year, in fact – the Dean made an interesting discovery. He found out that before Lord Caverner left the College, he secretly filled the Catacombs with booby traps to stop anyone from finding Edgar's body. *That* was the reason that no guests ever came back up from the Catacombs. They weren't being killed by the Jabberers! They were dying while searching for Edgar's tomb! Perhaps, thought the Dean, that whole part of the story was just a myth – perhaps *anyone* could take the Jabberers and wear them for themselves!

'There was nothing to stop the Dean from claiming the teeth – except for one small problem. When the other guests found out what the Dean had done, they would hunt him down and kill him. So he decided to get rid of them, once and for all. That year, at the annual Christmas Dinner of Souls, he served them all poisoned gin.'

The guests' eyes widened in horror. They stared down at their empty glasses. The Dean smiled.

'Would anyone like to guess what my course is?'

The guests looked at him, then at each other – and slumped onto the table, dead.

Lewis stood frozen to the spot. All fifty guests were lying face down in the last of their Christmas pudding. The Dean picked up his glass, sniffed it absent-mindedly, and threw it at the fireplace. The fumes caught in the flames and lit up the room like a furnace. Without missing a beat he strolled calmly towards Lady Arabella's dogs and expertly tied their leashes round a table leg.

'Forty years, I've been holding these dreadful dinners. Thanks for your help, boy – I couldn't have done it without you.'

Lewis flew towards the door. The Dean whipped a pistol from his jacket pocket.

'Not so fast! Your night's not over, boy – in fact, it's only just beginning . . . !'

The kitchen door creaked open and the Cook wandered into the dining room, carrying a tray of coffee served in human skulls. He made it halfway to the table before noticing the dead guests. He looked at the Dean – who was still pointing a gun at Lewis – and started shuffling backwards.

'Hold it right there!' cried the Dean, aiming the pistol at him. 'You're coming with us, freak! We have a job to do!'

He unbolted the trapdoor marked CATACOMBS and threw it open. A low moan of wind blew from the world beneath them; the air filled with the stench of death.

'The Dead Man's Jabberers are somewhere below us,' said the Dean. 'And I intend to find them. Forty years I've waited for this moment – and you two are going to be with me every step of the way!'

He kicked Lewis through the trapdoor,

and he hit the ground with a gasp. It was like being flung into an ice well. Lewis couldn't see a thing in the pitch black – the air was heavy and stale.

'Get down there, imbecile!'

There was the sound of a scuffle from above, and then the Cook slammed to the ground beside Lewis. He lay doubled up in pain, groaning weakly. The Dean landed nimbly beside them and held up a torch to the darkness.

Lewis gazed at the Catacombs – and gasped. It was a network of tunnels that seemed to run on for miles, holding up the College with ornate stone pillars. But when you looked closer, you realised they weren't pillars – they were cabinets for the dead. Each pillar held a dozen tombs, arranged in rows with their names carved into the stone.

'A thousand corpses,' said the Dean grimly.

'The whole College is built on them – and in one of them lies the body of Edgar Caverner. When we find him, we find the Dead Man's Jabberers. Then power and immortality are finally mine, all mine!'

The Dean's eyes shone hungrily in the torchlight. Lewis got to his knees and begged.

'Please, we won't tell anyone what happened! Just let us go!'

The Dean laughed. 'What – and let my two little canaries fly away? You heard what I said upstairs – these tunnels are filled with booby traps. I haven't come this far to end up falling into a pit of spikes or get crushed by a boulder – *you* have!' He aimed the gun at Lewis. 'You're going to walk ahead of me and set them off yourself!'

Lewis gasped. 'N–no! You can't do that!'

The Dean ignored him, and gave the Cook an almighty kick.

'Up you get, freak! Your time has come, too – I doubt anyone will miss you!'

The Cook gazed into the torchlight. Lewis was once again struck by his face – the one that looked like cold, cooked meat packed against his skull. The one that had terrified him so much at the beginning of the night. Now, after everything that Lewis had seen and heard, he realised that the Cook was the person he was least afraid of.

Without warning, the Cook leapt to his feet and shot down the tunnels. Lewis was surprised by how quickly he moved – so was the Dean.

'Hey, stop!' snapped the Dean. 'There's nowhere you can run to – come back here!'

But the Cook didn't stop. He threw his whole body forward, lurching with gasping breaths down the tunnels. He didn't seem to be worried about setting off any booby traps – he wasn't even limping any more. It was all

Lewis and the Dean could do to keep up with him.

'SLOW DOWN, YOU IDIOT!' cried the Dean, dragging Lewis by the wrist. 'You'll set off the traps! We're supposed to be checking every tomb as we go . . .'

The Cook kept running, twisting and turning through the labyrinth of pillars. He wasn't just running – he knew where he was going. He was leading them somewhere.

And suddenly he stopped. The Dean and Lewis screeched to a halt beside him.

'*You moron!* You could have gotten me killed!' The Dean pointed the gun at the Cook's head. 'This is my *one* chance to find the body of Edgar Caverner, and I'm not going to let some pasty-faced troll . . .'

He trailed off. The Cook was leaning on a pillar, heaving with ragged breaths. His greasy fingers rested on the handle of a tomb:

The Dean's mouth fell open – his eyes widened in disbelief. He gave a great yelp.

'I . . . I did it!' he cried, dancing for joy. 'I found Edgar's tomb! The Dead Man's Jabberers are mine at long last!'

Lewis glared at him. 'OK, you've found what you wanted. Now let us go!'

The Dean stopped dancing. 'Oh, I can't do *that*.'

He whipped back round with the pistol.

'You see, I don't plan on making the same mistake as Edgar. I'm going to make sure that once I have the Dead Man's Jabberers, no one can take them away from me ever again. I'm not leaving behind a single trace of their existence – not even stories. I've already killed the only fifty people in the world who know they exist. Well – make that fifty-two, once

I'm done with the both of you.'

The Dean pulled back the hammer on the pistol and gave them another cold smile in the darkness.

'Then I'm going to torch the whole College. The library is filled to the rafters with dynamite. In an hour's time, it'll all be gone. No one will miss it – least of all me. People will say that the College burned down tragically one Christmas morning – and there were no survivors. Not the Dean, not the staff, and certainly not one naughty, little boy.'

The Dean held the gun to Lewis's head and smirked.

'Tell me, boy, do you still wish you'd broken that window?'

The Dean stopped. There was a noise coming from behind him – the sound of muffled screams. The sound of someone pounding against a locked door.

'What— what is that?' said the Dean nervously. 'Where's that coming from?'

Lewis looked at the nearest pillar . . . and his stomach dropped. The sound was coming from the locked tombs. There were people inside them – they were kicking and screaming against the cabinet doors. The Dean's mouth fell open in horror.

'They . . . they're alive!' he cried. 'But how—'

'Oh, it's really quite easy when you know how.'

The Dean swung round. The Cook was still gazing up at him, the grey lumpen skin on his face twisted into a smile.

'That one beside you's been down here since last year. Poor Umberto Skelliosis! He thought he was certain *to find the teeth – but no such luck. The tomb above him? That's Alopecia Hike –* she's *been down here for at least twelve years now!'*

The Dean stumbled back in terror as the drawers beside him shuddered and screamed. The torch in his hand shook, making the light dance across the Cook's grey and greasy face.

'Who— who *are* you . . .'

The Cook stood up to his full height, releasing his back in a series of cracks. Now you could see that he was actually very tall and very thin. He reached up to his face, dug his fingers into the skin . . . and pulled away the flesh. It came off in great clumps, scattering like mincemeat onto the floor. Lewis gasped – it *was* mincemeat. Cold, cooked mincemeat packed into clumps against his skull. It was a mask, covering the face beneath it.

The face of a man who'd lived in the darkness all his life. The pale mad eyes, the grey hair.

The rotting teeth.

'*Surprised?*' said Edgar Caverner.

The Dean trembled from head to toe. 'B–but ... you died! Your father found your body and—'

'*Dean, Dean.*' Edgar laughed. '*Do you have any idea how easy it is to fake your own death? It was the only way to ensure no one would come looking for me – how else could I take part in these wonderful annual dinners for the rest of time?*'

The Dean was speechless with fear. Edgar sighed.

'*I must say, that was a rather impressive trick you pulled off upstairs – but it does make next year's dinner a bit of a problem. I'll have to start over again, I guess – find somewhere new. Of course,* you *won't be around to appreciate it . . .*'

The Dean lifted his pistol, but Edgar was too quick for him. He tore the gun from his hands and in one great swoop threw open the cabinet marked EDGAR CAVERNER and thrust the Dean inside. The Dean had just enough time to give a final shriek of terror before the drawer slammed shut, the lock turned, and his cries became one more muffled scream in the darkness.

Edgar Caverner chuckled.

'Wonderful night, wasn't it, boy? I must say, those dinners get better every year . . .'

Lewis wasn't there to hear him say it. He was flying back through the darkness of the Catacombs, back towards the trapdoor. He wouldn't stop running until he was out of the dining room and through the black gates and Soul's College was far behind him. On the far horizon the clock tower rang out the hour, seven chimes pounding out across the village rooftops. It was Christmas Day – darkness slipped away from the world once more, racing back to the secret corners of the earth, always waiting and always ready to return.

'I'll never be bad again!' Lewis cried into the dawn. 'I'll be good every day of my life – I swear it!'

By the time Lewis reached the edge of the forest, flames had already started flickering in the windows of the library. Soon the Dean's stashes of dynamite would explode, and Soul's College would be razed to the ground. Lewis stopped at the village, watching as the fire rose higher and higher. Even from down here, he swore he could still hear a voice on the wind.

It was the same voice that had chased him out of the Catacombs, shrieking from the darkness beneath Soul's College. The voice he would never forget until the day he died.

'Merry Christmas, boy!'

If you liked this, you'll love . . .